THE
WORLD'S
ONE HUNDRED
BEST SHORT STORIES

[IN TEN VOLUMES]

GRANT OVERTON
EDITOR - IN - CHIEF

VOLUME SIX
COURAGE

FUNK & WAGNALLS COMPANY
NEW YORK AND LONDON

CONTENTS

THE WORLD'S 100 BEST SHORT STORIES

THE TRUMPET SOUNDS

By Mary Roberts Rinehart

Big Joe Allison had shot his wife and cut his own throat. All the Fifth Ward had expected it for some time, except Anna Allison herself. But, then, the ward could have told her some things about Joe that she did not know: his slow quietness and then his occasional violences.

But the ward had not liked Anna, with her bobbed hair and her eyes traveling about looking for admiration. Always like that she was, with her slim legs in silk stockings twinkling along the streets and her challenging look and half smile.

No one was immune from those sly attacks of Anna's.

"Half a dozen eggs," she would say to the grocer, and look up at him from under her lashes. "And don't pick out the bantams. Joe's hollow all the way."

"Head and all, eh?"

"Oh, his head's solid enough," she would say, and laugh a little contemptuously. It was not long before all the ward knew that she had married Joe for reasons of her own, but that those reasons had nothing to do with love.

Mrs. Harrison, who lived above the poolroom across the street, sized her up quickly. "If you ask me," she said, "she's a hussy. And the sooner Joe finds it out the better."

But Anna was too shrewd for that. Joe would come home to a tidy flat, with Anna moving daintily about, and after the supper things were cleaned up he would take her on his knee and sit for a while, content just to hold her.

And Anna would submit. She had a way of running her hand up his sleeve and stroking his great arm, covered with strong, dark hair. "Are you still crazy about me, Joe?"

"You bet I am."

He paid her without question the tributes her vanity demanded. He saw in the tidy flat not a setting for Anna herself but a welcome home to a tired man; thought her fastidious care of her small body was to make it attractive to him, and without being conscious of it felt in her coolness and lack of passion a safeguard.

He did not know that vanity leads more women astray than love.

On Sunday mornings he crept out of bed and went to early mass without disturbing her. Anna had been a Protestant before her marriage, but she had changed her faith as easily as she had changed her name, and after a time Joe had given up trying to make a good Catholic of her.

"Now listen, boy," she would say. "I don't care about those things. They were left out of me, somehow. And I'll take what's coming to me in the next world. I'll be a sport all right when the time comes."

That was a favorite expression of hers. Being a sport was the nearest she had to a creed.

Now and then Father Murphy would meet her on the street. A big man was Father Murphy, corpulent and hoary, and an untidy man too for all his holiness. The very spots on his clothing endeared him to a district which could understand the slovenliness of a womanless man better than the preening daintiness of a married Anna. And when Father Murphy met Anna, on Wheeler Street it might be, or on the avenue by the church, Anna would dodge by if she could. When she could not she would stop and inspect him with cool appraisal. Not a spot missed her eyes. And when she finally looked up into his face it would be with a half smile, cynical and suspicious.

When Joe told her of the holiness and austerity of his life she openly sneered.

"Don't you believe it," she said. "He's a *man*, isn't he? I wouldn't trust him around the corner."

And Father Murphy, after a call or two, gave up going to see her. It was not only that she used most of the tricks she knew on him; it was because he felt that behind that young and slightly smiling face there was a wall of hardness that could not be broken down.

But Anna worried him. He began to see her on street corners talking to men, a little flushed, a trifle daring, and Joe off at work at the time. And there came a day when Joe went to see Father Murphy, sitting uncomfortably in the bare parlor and holding his hat on his knees, and asked for a little advice.

"She's young," he said, "and she means no harm. But she likes to play a bit, and people will begin to talk soon."

Father Murphy did the best he could, and in the end

Joe carried back with him a holy medal, which Anna laughed at and refused to wear. But the matter preyed on the father's mind. He could reach the generation he understood; not a domestic trouble in the ward for years but had been brought to him. But this new generation was beyond him.

One day he stopped at the bookshop on the avenue and carried home a book called "Practical Talks on Family Life." He marked some passages, such as: "A woman who dresses without propriety becomes an instrument of Satan," and so on. But how could one speak of propriety to an Anna who openly scoffed at it, or of Satan to one who feared neither God nor devil?

But as time went on and gossip began to reach him he sent to Anna a summons she dared not disobey.

She went in, defiant and wary, and her skirts were shorter and her stockings thinner than ever before. And Father Murphy saw her, not as she was, but as the product of evil loose in the world, and pityingly put a hand on her shoulder.

"My child," he began. But Anna twitched her shoulder away from him.

"I'll thank you to keep your hands off me," she said, and opening her cheap vanity case with hands that trembled began to paint her lips.

After that, what could he do? He talked to her— of a wife's duty to her husband and such like matters— but she had come armored against him, and never once did he penetrate that armor.

What he did after that it is not easy for a Protestant to understand. He seems to have taken the matter considerably to heart and to have worried more over this one lamb who had gone astray than over the ninety and nine. But Anna went her way, not knowing and not caring. Until the fever came.

How it came nobody knows. It had not visited the Fifth Ward for so long that it found a quarter totally unprepared. And it spread like an evil wind, knocking down here a man, there a woman, again a child. In the red brick hospital around the corner on the avenue the beds were filled in no time, and cots were spread down the center of the ward. The odor of fever hung over these wards, heavy and fetid. It moved in the flutter of nurses' skirts or to the opening of windows, only to settle again like a germ-laden fog, under which lips dried and bodies twisted and fingers picked at counterpanes.

Screens were moved about, and from behind them came the sickly sweetness of alcohol baths. Feeding cups sat on bedside stands, yellowish rims of dried milk within them. Probationers went around cleansing cracked and dried mouths with glycerine and myrrh, and up in the mortuary lay rows of sheeted bodies, neatly washed, each with the hands devoutly crossed and the jaw tied up with a bandage.

The mortuary was built like a chapel, and when the early morning sunlight flickered in through the windows, which had been covered with colored paper to look like stained glass, it gave an appearance of life to the still faces. Like a resurrection.

Father Murphy was in and out of the hospital at all hours with his shabby black bag. The nurses would place a screen around the bed and a clean towel on the bedside stand, and there Father Murphy would lay out what was essential. And sometimes after he had administered the sacrament he would follow the little procession to the mortuary and stay there to pray. He would wait outside until the nurses had finished and then ask humbly for admission.

"If I am not in the way, my child."

They were all his children: the nurses, the quick and the dead.

He slept but little, and what with work and fasting and prayer Joe and Anna somehow receded into the back of his mind. When Lent began, on Ash Wednesday, in his purple cope he blessed the ashes.

"Remember, man, that thou art dust! Scarcely does life begin when death approaches."

And the church seemed to be filled with grief.

"Look death in the face, and thou shalt not sin." And once more the wave of woe and desolation, for the Fifth Ward knew it had sinned and that now indeed it looked death in the face.

Joe was there, but Anna, of course, was not.

Time went on. Father Murphy grew thin; his coat hung almost straight in front, and his ruddy cheeks dropped in two dewlaps over his collar. One night, going down Walter's Alley, he heard a faint tapping on the glass of Aaron Kahn's tailor shop—"Ladies' and Gents' Repairing and Pressing"—and breaking in the door himself carried the stricken little Jew to the hospital.

The night porter was asleep, and they can show you to-day the marks on the door where Father Murphy kicked it open.

And then one day Joe Allison came to see him again.

The father was sitting still when he entered. He had not felt well for some time, and now his tongue was dried in his head and his eyes were burning in their sockets. But Joe, sitting white-faced across from him, knew neither of those things.

"I guess I'm kinda up against it Father," said Joe. "It's about Anna I'm speaking."

"I'm sorry to hear that, my son," said Father Murphy, with his tongue clacking against the roof of his mouth. He felt very dizzy. "If she would come to me now, and I'd give her a bit of a talk—"

"It's beyond that," said Joe. "She's got a fellow. I followed her last night when she thought I was working. I haven't been home since. If I go back I'll kill her, Father. I'm afraid to go back."

"I listen to no such talk as that," said Father Murphy sternly and with an effort. "She's young and foolish, but if she has done a wickedness it is no time for her to face her God. You hear me, Joe? I'll go myself." And he tried to get up, but there was a numbness in his legs and he could not move.

"I'll go myself," he said once more, and there was Joe, all clouded in a dark mist and then disappearing altogether. Father Murphy made one more effort, and then collapsed entirely.

Joe stayed around as long as he could. Sprinkled cold water, as one might know he would, got a doctor and later an ambulance, and only faced his own trouble again when Father Murphy was neatly tucked into a hard, smooth bed in Ward C, with a screen around him, because there were no private rooms vacant.

Aaron Kahn was in the next bed.

Joe went home that night. Anna was sitting alone in the dark, and she said nothing when he went in. He turned on the light, and he saw she had been crying, but he did not speak to her. He went into the bedroom and went to bed.

After a long time she came creeping in and lay on the edge far away from him. She did it so quietly that she might not have been there at all, except that the bed trembled when she sobbed. But after a while she moved over to him, and ran her hand up and down his arm. Joe's very soul shook under that touch.

"I'm not bad, Joe," she said. "Honest to God, Joe. I just went in there to Casey's for a minute. I came right out. You ask *him.*"

"Him" was the man she had been with.

"Then he saw me. I thought he did."

"No! Honest, Joe, I'm telling the truth. I was scared, Joe. I'm scared now. You act so queer."

"I'm thinking," said Joe, and freed his arm.

They set up some sort of a *modus vivendi* after that. Anna stayed in the flat, but after she had straightened it for the day there was nothing to fill in the time. She hated books. Mostly, according to Mrs. Harrison, she stood at a window and looked down at the street. And when Joe came home at night it was to sit under the chandelier in the tiny parlor and read the papers. But he did not read them; mostly he held the page before him and continued to think.

Twice a week, on visiting days, he went to the hospital and sat behind the screen beside Father Murphy's bed. But the father did not know him. Yet— and here was a strange thing—he kept asking for Joe. Joe and Anna.

"I'm here, Father," Joe would say. "What is it?"

"Joe," he would repeat. "Joe and Anna."

It may be that he had carried that last conscious

thought of his over the border with him. Or it may be—but who are we to deal in such matters?

And when Joe had gone he would still ask for him.

Except for that the father was fairly quiet. Aaron Kahn, reporting on the matter later, says that he mostly thought he was a boy again in Ireland and that the stars outside the window over his head were shining down on Iar Connacht and twinkling on Wicklow Woods.

And also that on one very clear night he sat up in his bed and said: "He is born, my children," thinking perhaps that the stars were the Christmas candles shining in the windows of Ireland, to guide the Christ child to each cabin and home. That seems probable, because when a wind came up and closed the door of the ward just after that he heard it and began to whimper. Strange to think of Father Murphy whimpering.

"They cannot come in," he said, with his dried tongue. "The Mother and Child are abroad to-night, and ye have closed the door."

One sees how far he was beyond Joe's reach when on visiting days he sat by the bed with his trouble, and the father babbled on. It was as tho the only hand Joe could hold to had drawn itself away.

"Don't you know me, Father?"

"Aroon, aroon, Soggarth, aroon," would mutter Father Murphy, back in the past and out of reach entirely.

And so things were when there came a day when Joe, reporting for work, was laid off indefinitely, and when he went home at noon to find the bed unmade, the breakfast dishes still in the sink and Anna out.

He went across the street and took up a position in

the window of the pool parlor, and he drank some bootleg whisky when it was offered to him. He had had nothing to drink since his marriage, and it destroyed the last inhibition in him, altho on the surface he was cool enough.

At four o'clock he saw Anna slipping home. He gave her an hour and then went back; the place was in order by that time, and Anna said she had not been out all day.

Joe caught her by the arms and shook her.

"Look up at me," he said. "Look up at me and repeat that lie."

And when she could not he got his old army revolver from a table drawer and shot her with the last bullet in it. Then he saw what he had done, and he tried to shoot himself. But the hammer came down with a futile click, and there was Joe still alive, and Anna on the floor.

It was then that he cut his throat.

What matters here, however, is what Aaron Kahn has to say about the matter. For at five o'clock by the C Ward clock, which is the time the Wilkins family in the flat below heard the shot, Aaron says that Father Murphy suddenly roused out of a stupor and sat up in his bed.

"What was that?" he said in a sharp tone.

Aaron, who was convalescing, leaned over and drew aside the loose muslin of the screen.

"It's all right, Father," he said. "Lie down or they'll be putting the bandages on you again."

The bandages, Aaron explained, were to hold Father Murphy in his bed because when he thought he was a boy again he would get out of it.

"'Tis Joe!" said the father, staring straight ahead of him. "Joe and Anna, his wife. May God have mercy on their souls!"

From that moment Aaron knew, he says, that something was wrong between Joe Allison and Anna.

Fifteen minutes later the bell of the patrol wagon was heard ringing furiously outside, and, still with the thought of Joe and Anna in his mind, Aaron sent the McNamara boy, who was able to get about, to inquire.

"Go and find out," he said. "The father here is worrying. See who came in."

So the McNamara boy, nothing loath, wandered down the corridor. At last he saw a policeman from the station house near by on guard outside a door and sitting on a radiator.

"And what's brought you here, Mister O'Leary?" said the McNamara boy. "God knows, 'tis here a fellow should be safe from the law, if anywhere."

"It's the truth," said O'Leary. "And when the Fifth Ward learns that, maybe a peaceful man like meself can have some rest."

The McNamara boy cocked an inquiring eye at the door.

"Is that so?" he said. "And you'll be claiming now that it's one of us in there at this minute, maybe."

"I'm not saying."

"Come on and tell me," said the McNamara boy, beginning to wheedle. "Come on, now! Who is it, and what's their trouble?"

O'Leary grinned and weakened.

"I *might* do that thing," he agreed, "if a smart boy like yourself knows of a spot handy where a man can take a puff of a cigaret without a nurse smacking it out of his face."

The news spread like wildfire through the hospital that evening. Joe Allison had shot his wife and cut his own throat.

But at Aaron Kahn's bed it stopped. Not so much as a whisper did Aaron let that dire news penetrate beyond the screen. Yet all that evening the father groaned like a soul in purgatory and gave answer to unheard questions. It was, C Ward says, as tho the holy angels had brought him the matter and laid it before him.

"Awake, Father Murphy, for there is trouble to-day. Joe Allison has shot his wife, Anna, and cut his own throat."

"And what shall I be doing then? I am a sick man, and my legs tremble under me if I stand."

"Go and save them," maybe they said, for he would reply, "Aye, Lord, I come," and try to get out of his bed. Aaron had to put him back over and over for fear the nurses would bring the bandages. . . .

They had taken Joe and Anna to the emergency ward.

The first thing the nurse on duty there had known of the tragedy was when she heard outside in the hall the familiar shuffling of feet. All policemen know how to carry stretchers and not to keep step.

So she had just time to whisk the white counterpanes off the two beds, leaving their gray woolen blankets ready, and the flat hard pillow with its rubber cover under the slip, when they were brought in.

She knew immediately that this was no ordinary case, for the patrolmen dumped Joe on his bed without ceremony. Not that Joe was conscious, but still—there it was. And by the different manner in which they lifted

Anna to hers, altho it made no difference to Anna either just then.

"Don't bother about *him*," one of them said. "Here's where your work is, sister. She's pretty bad, I'm thinking."

And Anna was indeed "pretty bad," altho Joe was nothing to write home about either. Finally the policemen went away, taking their rolled-up stretchers with them, and for some time there they lay, the two of them, side by side. They might almost have been in their bed at home. Even then Anna was appealing, and it seems rather a pity she could not have seen the admiration she was arousing. But nobody paid any particular attention to Joe, except an interne who was new and enthusiastic, and O'Leary, who was feeling sick like, but who couldn't leave. O'Leary's job was to see that Joe did not escape the gallows by dying prematurely.

"I'll hang around a while," he said. "If the girl says anything, you might call me; I'll be outside."

He did not include Joe, it being clear that Joe would not say anything at all for a long time.

So O'Leary went outside for a breath of air, and inside the emergency room the interne cut Joe's sleeve open to give him a hypodermic. And Joe roused and thought it was Anna, touching his arm as she used to. What with one thing and another, the slate of his mind was wiped clean of the last few weeks, and so he reached up and patted her hand, his eyes closed.

"Y' all right, honey?" he tried to say. But of course he could not speak.

After a while they separated them, Anna to a woman's ward, where, like Father Murphy, she was screened off. But hospitals use screens in several ways,

and so they were for Anna to die behind. And Joe
to the operating-room to be saved for the law.

And back in their flat Mrs. Harrison and the woman
from the apartment beneath straightened things up, all
very neat and nice. Indeed, there are some who say
that it was Mrs. Harrison who did away with Joe's
revolver, carrying it across the street in the leg of her
stocking. One thing is certain: there was no revolver
there when the officers came to examine the flat. True,
she never blinked an eye when she was accused of it,
and was willing to swear on a stack of Bibles a foot
high that she had not seen it. But the ward suspects
her.

However, it did not look as tho that or anything
else would save Joe if Anna died.

All that was on Wednesday.

The end of Lent was approaching. Already the drug
store at the corner of Wheeler Street and Walter's
Alley was selling envelopes of egg dyes, and in the
windows of some of the houses were bowls of them, red
and yellow and blue. All colors.

Wagons came into the market square at dawn each
morning and set out on the pavements their lilies and
their hyacinths, their tulips and narcissuses, carefully
wrapped against the early cold. When the sun rose
high enough they were uncovered, and then the children
who had been sewed into their flannels at the first frost
ran home to be cut out of them.

"It's warm, like summer," they pleaded. "And the
flowers are out."

The Fifth Ward saw few flowers except at Easter.

But there was little real joy in the ward, what with

the fever and all. And every day the news from the hospital was poor.

"Have you heard how's the father today?"

"He's getting weaker, they're saying."

When on top of that came the tragedy of Joe and Anna, a wave of superstitious terror passed over the district. Sure, then, and the powers of darkness must be loose among them. And there were still three days to go. Three days until the feast of feasts and the end of sorrow and penance. Three days until Easter.

That Wednesday night many of the people made a pilgrimage downtown to the cathedral to pray. It seemed to them that God was perhaps more likely to be there, seeing that their own church was as it was and the ward very likely in disrepute above.

When they got there they slipped in very humbly. And when, during the service, the organ sank into hopeless grief and the candles were extinguished one by one, it seemed to them they could not bear it. At last only one candle remained, and when it had been taken behind the altar and hidden there, it seemed as tho their hearts would break.

The Light of the World had gone out. Come back, O Light of the World, and bring us hope again, and peace and mercy.

They waited breathlessly. The church was very still, and then the light returned once more.

Joe lay that night in his bed in the men's surgical ward. He had to breathe through a tube in his throat, and sometimes the tube filled up. Then the sound of Joe's breathing filled the room.

He had no time to think. All he could do was to get air into his lungs and then get it out again. Breathe.

Let it out. Breathe. Let it out. All day and all night.

But he was conscious. If a man might die by hold-ing his breath, he would have died. But he could not; he who so wished to die must make his fight for life. Breathe. Let it out. Breathe. Let it out. Oh, God!

The men around him could not sleep. When the nurse came in to clean the tube they muttered their protests or sat up to slap and turn viciously their crumpled pillows.

Joe dared not sleep. Hardly he dared to close his eyes. Air. Air. Open the windows. God, open the windows!

Anna, on the other hand, was quite comfortable. She was not greatly interested in where she was or why she was there. All she wanted was to look at the dirty gray of the ceiling overhead or at the white muslin of her screens and to be let alone.

But something would not let her alone. This some-thing was a voice, and just when she was most com-fortable it insisted on asking her a question.

"Was it Joe? *Was it Joe? Was it Joe?*" It said it over and over.

When it became really annoying, all easy as she was, she turned her head, and there was a man with a note-book beside her.

"Was it Joe?" he said again.

"Was what Joe?"

"Who shot you?"

Ah, that was it; she had known there was something, but she had forgotten it in this new peace. Joe had shot her, and now maybe she was going to—She put that away. It was unpleasant.

"What about Joe?" she asked slowly.

"It was Joe did this, wasn't it?"

So that was it too! The dirty dog, trying to make trouble! What had happened was her business and Joe's and for nobody else. There was a queer, mocking look in the eyes she turned on the officer.

"You'd like to know, wouldn't you!" she scoffed in a whisper.

"We know all right."

"Then get out of here and quit bothering me. I want to sleep."

"But it *was* Joe, wasn't it?"

"Oh, get the h— out of here," said Anna wearily. "If you want to know, I did it myself. Take that away and dream on it!" And when he sat back and snapped his notebook shut she smiled faintly. "I did it myself, with my—little hatchet," she added breathlessly.

Just before two o'clock the man went away defeated, and the nurse came in and took a look at Anna. Then she went out again and looked at Anna's card: "Sex, female; color, white; age, twenty; religion, R. C."

"Roman Catholic," she reflected. "I'd better get a priest."

But when she proposed this to Anna she only shook her head.

"What's the use?" she said, without bitterness. "I'll take—I'll take what's coming to me." And lapsed into her comfortable stupor again.

But Aaron Kahn insists that she had a priest that night, and that the priest was Father Murphy. And it is well known that the nurses found a rosary in her hands. They tried to take it away, so they could work around her better, but she would not let it go.

In every hospital there are periods of ebb and full tide.

The full tide is at four or so in the afternoon; the ebb begins after midnight, when vitality grows low and resistance weakens. It is then that the temperature charts, which have perhaps been showing high points like the peaks of a mountain range, suddenly begin to go down into the Valley of the Shadow. The line slants; it gets to the safety point, but it does not stop there. It goes down and down—and then perhaps it ceases.

So even at the beginning of the ebb tide that night Father Murphy was very weak. He lay in his bed and looked out at the stars as they used to shine down on Iar Connacht or twinkle on Wicklow Woods, but this time they seemed different to him.

He appeared to think that they were the lights on an altar. And of course so they may be, but who are we to say?

But after a time a fog came up and one by one the stars went out until only one was left. All of C Ward heard him groan when that last star was extinguished and speak despairingly aloud:

"The Light of the World has gone out. And I am a worm and no man; the reproach of men and the outcast of people."

But only Aaron the Jew knew that from that moment he lay waiting for its return again or was aware of the great sigh of relief he gave when it came.

"Now have mercy and hope returned to the world," said Father Murphy sonorously, "and I must go about my Father's business."

Aaron heard a soft movement behind the screen and knew what it portended. He stuck his feet into his old slippers and got up, but he was too late. Father Murphy was standing beside his bed, swaying slightly,

and the next minute he was pushing past Aaron and
out into the ward.

"Y'understand," Aaron says, in telling the story, "if
I let him go and the nurse finds out, I get hell, see?
So I ain't taking no chances."

So Aaron caught him by the arm and tried to hold
him, but the father shook him off. He seemed amazingly strong all at once. He went straight down the
ward and out of the door—just as he was, night garments and bare feet and all. Aaron was frightened
almost out of his wits, but he did the best he could—
flung a blanket around his shoulders and caught up
another for the father, and then followed him into
the hall.

For what came after we have only Aaron's word.
It seems fairly incredible that those two, Aaron, the
Jew, and the priest, could have made their excursion
unseen. Yet there is certain evidence to uphold it; for
example, Aaron speaks of the odor of boiling coffee in
one of the halls. He always says: "They were cooking
coffee, you know," and then looks around, as if to a
situation he cannot somehow make real—the coffee is
the one real thing to which he clings.

But the coffee for the night nurses' supper is cooked
far from C Ward, in the women's wing.

Still, there are some things which Aaron may have
added later; that about the restless men growing quiet
in C Ward as the father passed through it is one;
and another is about that stop at the door of Joe's
ward, and the father's lifted hand and the word
"Peace." At which Joe's breathing grew quieter, and
he slept.

But, however that may be, it seems certain that

Father Murphy got to Anna Allison that night, and that there he wrestled for some time with the devil for the prize of Anna's obstinate, unshriven little soul. How long he stayed we do not know. Aaron, left at the door of the ward, says it was long enough, what with one thing and another.

"And me in my night shirt, y'understand," he says plaintively. "Twice I had to hide in a bathroom, and I guess I should maybe kiss myself good-by, if they caught me there, eh? I'm telling you!"

However, nobody found him, and finally Father Murphy came back along the darkened ward. He was apparently still quite strong and full of life, and together they made that strange return journey of theirs, during which the father paused only once, and then at a window. He stood there looking out, and then he said, like a man pleading:

"O Jerusalem, Jerusalem! Return to the Lord thy God."

Then he went on, and in the morning he was dead.

Nobody had told Joe whether Anna lived or not, and at first it made no difference, because he was not thinking. But after the first few hours he began to think, and then every time the nurse came to clean out the tube he formed the word with his lips.

"Anna," he would try to say. "Anna?"

But the nurse would only shake her head.

"You mustn't try to talk," she would say.

By the second day he could look around the room, with eyes haunted by deadly terror. Anna? Had he killed Anna? But no one replied to that look. No one, indeed, came near him. The small services of the ward were not for him, nor its kindnesses. In its dragging carpet slippers, on crutches or in wheeled chairs, the ward passed and repassed his bed; it stared and commented. But it avoided him.

He made signals to them, and they ignored him. But finally, on the second day that was, a boy came and stood beside the bed.

"What is it you want?" he said. "Nurse? Orderly?"

"My wife?" said Joe with his lips, and staring up with his tortured eyes. "Is she alive?"

"Here, Karl," called the boy across the ward. "Lend us your pencil. Maybe he can write it."

But Karl raised himself in his bed and glowered across at Joe.

"I lend no pencil to a murderer," he snarled, and lay back again.

So sure was Joe then that Anna was gone that it made little difference to him after that when he saw the ward humorist gesturing toward his bed and then strangling himself with his hands as with a rope.

It was the same officer who had approached Anna who got his confession from him. Joe offered no difficulties; he nodded "yes" to the questions and even feebly scrawled his name to the paper he was offered.

Then, as if there was still a flicker of hope in him, he tried to write his desperate query beneath his signature. But the pencil fell out of his fingers, and for the first and only time Joe wept.

He lay there, helpless as a baby, and great tears rolled down his cheeks. The officer thought he was weeping for himself!

Good Friday by that time, and the Fifth Ward in double mourning; the shades in Father Murphy's little house drawn, and by afternoon the people flocking to the church, where no lights burned on the altar and hope seemed gone indeed.

Up one aisle and down the other they went to see Father Murphy lying in state in his church. And outside on the pavement a tale was whispered about, that Aaron the Jew had told: of how he had risen from his bed to save the soul of Anna Allison and had paid this price for that soul.

"He was a good man and holy," they said. "And he died for that strumpet. Evil she came, and evil may she go."

They hoped that she would die.

But Father Murphy lay, very comfortable and majestic, in the light of the candles. Like a man who has earned his rest!

With Saturday, however, things began to brighten up a little. The father, after all, had not been young, and he had died full of good works and saintliness. Little pots of flowers began to come into the hospital, to be distributed in the wards, and the voices of the choir boys at the Episcopal Mission, practising their Easter anthem, floated in at the open windows.

It was warm too and sunny. When the men came along the streets outside to clear the fire plugs of their winter deposit of mud, the children took off their shoes and stockings and splashed in the gutters.

But best of all, the fever was receding. The night nurses at the hospital no longer came off duty exhausted to drag themselves to their beds; there was time properly to clean the feeding cups, to put in order the medicine closets, to fold and tidy the sheets.

The long, sad season was over. Soon could the world arise from its knees and go about its business.

All but Joe and Anna, his wife.

Anna was never out of Joe's thoughts; never did the
nurse rouse him with a touch on the arm that he did
not think it was Anna, and never did he come to full
consciousness without dying a thousand deaths of remorse. He had loved her terribly. He knew now that,
good or bad as she might have been, he still loved her.

And somehow he saw too, in that new clairvoyance
of his, that she had loved him. How far she had wandered he did not know; it seemed now not to matter.
She had come back to him, a little frightened, perhaps
wary and defiant, but she had come back.

She had come back, and he had killed her.

Anna, Anna!

Anna knew that she was dying. There was no de-
ceiving her. She watched the nurses' faces with eyes
that, if sunken, were still shrewd.

"Am I—bad?"

"You're doing fine."

"You're—lying to me."

They had not told her about Joe. But on Holy
Saturday toward evening she asked for him.

"I'd like to see Joe," she said.

"Well, maybe we can arrange that later," said the
nurse briskly, and looked away. "But you'd better rest
now."

"I'd like to tell him—something."

"Can't you tell me?"

"No."

She lay still and closed her eyes, but her mind was
evidently busy, for a little later she called the nurse back.

"I guess—I'd better not see him—after all," she said,
with that new breathlessness which had bothered her
all day.

She had been thinking it over, you see, and of course she could not see Joe. He would give it all away, and then the law would get him. After that she only spoke once that evening. Then she muttered something about being a sport, but the nurse did not get it.

She began to sink after that. The line on the chart on the nurse's desk outside began to drop at nine o'clock; Anna's face was cold and pinched, and her hands were clammy. But she still held to her rosary; it was, in a sense, all she had to cling to.

She felt lonely, dying there like that, but she did not fool herself. She had deserved it. She had had Joe, and she had thrown him away. He hated her or he would be with her now. It had never entered her sick mind that Joe might not be able to come to her.

All she knew was that she wanted him and he was not there.

Toward midnight an interne came and gave her a hypodermic, and the touch of his strong hands roused her.

"Honest to God, Joe!" she muttered. "I only went—"

It looked then as tho Anna, rosary and all, was going to die with a lie on her lips.

At midnight some Negroes passed along the street below. Their soft voices rose, plaintive, beseeching and said:

> 'Tain't my mother or my father,
>   But it's me, O Lord,
> Standin' in the need of prayer.
>   It's me, it's me, it's me, O Lord,
> An' I'm standin' in the need of prayer. . . .

But Anna did not hear them.

So was Easter ushered into the Fifth Ward that night, with things as to Joe and Anna about as bad as they could be; with joy tempered with sorrow in the houses, the larders filled, the alarm clocks set for the early mass; with Father Murphy lying in his church in the candlelight, and a guard of honor to watch by him; and with Aaron the Jew, to whom it was not Easter Eve at all but Saturday night, sleepless in his bed and low in his mind.

And it is from Aaron the Jew that we must construct the rest of the story.

Briefly, Aaron says that he was lying in his bed, awake, and Father Murphy's bed was empty and neat and square beside him. Aaron was wide awake, and he cites the Negroes' singing as a proof of it:

> It's me, it's me, it's me, O Lord,
> I'm standin' in the need of prayer.

Then, Aaron says, all at once there was the heavy fragrance of flowers in the air, such as filled the church that night, and mixed in with it was the odor of incense—altho how Aaron recognized the incense it is not for us to know.

He sat up in his bed, and all was as it had been. The McNamara boy was snoring, and somebody down the ward rapped on his stand with his tin cup. Which everybody knows is a signal to the nurse outside for water.

So Aaron lay down again, and turned so he faced that empty bed in the dark corner. And the corner was not dark, nor was the bed empty.

Father Murphy was in the bed, just as if—well,

just as if nothing had happened. Only he looked very
peaceful and quiet, and his hands were crossed on his
breast and held a crucifix. Aaron saw him plainly,
because there was a Light.

"What sort of light? Candles?"

"Well, maybe. I ain't sure. But there was a light,
tho. I seen it. But maybe it came from the star."

"What star?"

"The star he was always looking at," he explained
patiently. "The one he called the Light of the World."

However all that may be, it is what followed that
matters. For Aaron says that while he looked at him
Father Murphy sat up in his bed, and first he glanced
out of the window and then he looked at Aaron and
spoke.

"He is risen," he said, and looked at Aaron as if
daring him to deny it. But Aaron did not. Instead he
said in a trembling voice—and how the words came
to him he does not know:

"He is risen indeed."

The father seemed to be relieved at that answer and
was quiet for a moment or so, according to Aaron.
Then he said:

"I have gone away and left my work undone, and
my soul has no rest. Arise you, Aaron, and go to
Anna Allison. Lay your hands on her wound and say
to her that she must not die or evil will come of it."

"Now?" said Aaron, shaking.

"Now," said the father.

So Aaron got up and drew on his old hospital trousers—he had been promoted, as one may say, to trousers
by that time—and stuck his feet in his slippers. But
he would not turn his back to that bed next to his or
to what it contained.

When he was ready to go he looked at the father
again. He was still much as he had been, but not so
clear to be seen. "Fading" is Aaron's word for it, and
it is as good as any. And he spoke once more, but
very faintly now.

"Go to Joe also," he said, "and tell him that Anna—"

He never finished it, because just then the Negroes
outside started to sing again:

> My Lord, he calls me,
> He calls me by the thunder.
> The trumpet sounds within—my soul.

And there was Aaron, standing in his trousers and
slippers beside the bed in the corner and nothing in
it at all.

Aaron felt very odd, like a man rudely awakened
from a sleep—as of course he may have been. His
first impulse was to go back to his couch and do
nothing.

"My knees were like water," he says, and adds:
"And the bed was smooth, you know." He looks at
one wistfully when he says this; it is to explain his
moment of weakness.

But in the end he decided to go.

He had far more trouble than the two of them had
had before. At one time he dodged into a closet and
some pans fell down with a fearful crash; and again
he only escaped the night watchman by getting out
on a fire escape. But in the end he got to Anna's
ward and slid inside.

He knew where to go well enough, but there was a
woman awake and moving about in it and a nurse with

Anna herself. It looked bad, and if the nurse had not gone out it might have been hopeless.

But she went out (it was to write "Pulse indistinguishable" on Anna's record, as a matter of fact) and so Aaron finally got in.

"Anna," he said, "Anna!"

She looked up at him, and once more she thought it was Joe.

"I'm glad you've come," she said in her half whisper. "I never blamed you. I—"

"Now see here, Anna," Aaron said in a businesslike tone. "You gotta get well. Don't you know that?"

Well, she saw then that it was not Joe, and she turned sulky.

"I don't want to," she said. "Go away—and let me alone."

"All right," said Aaron, "if that's the way you feel about it. Let Joe hang. It's not my business."

"Hang?" said Anna. "What do you mean—hang? It's—my fault, isn't it?"

"The law should think of that!"

"But I told them—"

"Forget it," said Aaron. "They've got the goods on him. You better get well and be quick about it."

Then some recollection seems to have come to him that he had twisted his message somewhat and forgotten a part of it. For he put his hands, awkwardly one may be sure, on her bandaged body and held them there for a minute.

"You get well, girl," he said. "You're all right, and we're for you, y'understand?"

And Anna nodded submissively, as if indeed she did.

Having thus completed, if somewhat crudely, his apostolic mission, Aaron went away again. Not far, however, for he was discovered outside the ward door, and the next morning, Easter, he was sent home. They brought him his clothes tied up in a wrinkled bundle and got from the office his two dollars and ten cents in money, and turned him out.

But he had saved Anna Allison, and through her he had saved Joe.

The ward let him alone that Easter Day, save for some little boys who threw stones at his window because it was Easter and Aaron was a Jew. And Aaron feebly swept up the broken glass and made no protest.

That afternoon, however, he pressed his clothes and ventured back to the hospital, feebly, as befitted his condition, but sturdily as befitted his purpose, to see Joe.

"How're you feeling?" he asked. "Better? Well, that's all right."

He was filled with great thoughts, but in the unfriendly eyes of the surgical ward he stood awkward and uncomfortable.

"Treatin' you pretty good?"

But Joe did not answer. He was trying to say something. Aaron leaned down over the bed and studied his lips, and it was Aaron who understood.

"Anna?" he said. "Well, they're kinda tight down in the office, but I was talkin' by the doctor himself. She's better to-day. She's doin' good. You just forget it and get well."

Life goes on much as usual in the Fifth Ward. They still sell bad liquor in the shed behind the poolroom, and the new priest who has taken Father Murphy's place cannot stop it. And Anna still goes up and down

Wheeier Street, her slim legs in silk stockings and her eyes glancing about for admiration.

Not at once do you change the Annas of the world.

But she no longer stops at the corners, a little flushed, a trifle daring, to talk to the men gathered there. The men are afraid, for one thing, and perhaps so is Anna. When Joe comes home at night she crawls on his lap, and Joe holds her there.

"Are you still crazy about me, Joe?"

"You bet I am," he says. But he has to free one hand to say it, for Joe still had to cover the end of his tube before he can speak.

The ward has never quite believed Aaron's story. Mostly they think he slept and dreamed it, for the guard of honor that night at the church says his reverence never moved during the night, and all was as it should be.

Only one man says different, and he speaks of a cold wind at midnight, but perhaps somebody had opened a door. But two things bear him out. The fever began to die that night and has not come back again; and there is the matter of O'Leary the policeman, last Easter Eve.

And a hard-headed man is O'Leary.

It was like this:

O'Leary was gumshoeing down Walter's Alley looking for bootleggers when what should he hear but a strange sound from Aaron's shop, "Ladies' and Gents' Pressing and Repairing."

So O'Leary stopped to listen, and there it was: Tap-tap-tap.

So O'Leary, who is a bold man, walked on his rubber heels to Aaron's shop and tried the door, and as it was open he went in. And what should be there but Aaron, curled up in the window place and tapping on the glass! Tap-tap-tap, tap-tap-tapping away for dear life.

It was dark in there, so Aaron never saw O'Leary until he was inside. And it was then that Aaron gave a sort of cry and stretched out his arms like a man who had waited long and hungrily.

"I knew you would come again, Father," he said, and dropped in a faint.

THE MATADOR OF THE FIVE TOWNS

By Arnold Bennett

Chapter I

Mrs. Brindley looked across the lunch-table at her husband with glinting, eager eyes, which showed that there was something unusual in the brain behind them.

"Bob," she said, factitiously calm. "You don't know what I've just remembered!"

"Well?" said he.

"It's only grandma's birthday to-day!"

My friend Robert Brindley, the architect, struck the table with a violent fist, making his little boys blink, and then he said quietly:

"*The* deuce!"

I gathered that grandmama's birthday had been forgotten and that it was not a festival that could be neglected with impunity. Both Mr. and Mrs. Brindley had evidently a humorous appreciation of crises, contretemps, and those collisions of circumstances which are usually called "junctures" for short. I could have imagined either of them saying to the other: "Here's a funny thing! The house is on fire!" And then yielding to laughter as they ran for buckets. Mrs. Brindley, in particular, laughed now; she gazed at the table-cloth and laughed almost silently to herself; tho it appeared that their joint forgetfulness might result in temporary estrangement from a venerable

ancestor who was also, birthdays being duly observed,
a continual fount of rich presents in specie.

Robert Brindley drew a time-table from his breast-
pocket with the rapid gesture of habit. All men of
business in the Five Towns seem to carry that time-
table in their breast-pockets. Then he examined his
watch carefully.

"You'll have time to dress up your progeny and catch
the 2:05. It makes the connection at Knype for Axe.

The two little boys, aged perhaps four and six, who
had been ladling the messy contents of specially deep
plates on to their bibs, dropped their spoons and began
to babble about gray-granny, and one of them insisted
several times that he must wear his new gaiters.

"Yes," said Mrs. Brindley to her husband, after reflection. "And a fine old crowd there'll be in the train
—with this foot-ball match!"

"Can't be helped! . . . Now you kids, hook it
upstairs to nurse."

"And what about you?" asked Mrs. Brindley.

"You must tell the old lady I'm kept by business."

"I told her that last year, and you know what
happened."

"Well," said Brindley. "Here Loring's just come.
You don't expect me to leave him, do you? Or have
you had the beautiful idea of taking him over to Axe
to pass a pleasant Saturday afternoon with your esteemed grandmother?"

"No," said Mrs. Brindley. "Hardly that!"

"Well, then?"

The boys, having first revolved on their axes, slid
down from their high chairs as tho from horses.

"Look here," I said. "You mustn't mind me. I
shall be all right."

"Ha-ha!" shouted Brindley. "I seem to see you turned loose alone in this amusing town on a winter afternoon. I seem to see you!"

"I could stop in and read," I said, eyeing the multitudinous books on every wall of the dining-room. The house was dadoed throughout with books.

"Rot!" said Brindley.

This was only my third visit to his home and to the Five Towns, but he and I had already become curiously intimate. My first two visits had been occasioned by official pilgrimages as a British Museum expert in ceramics. The third was for a purely friendly week-end, and had no pretext. The fact is, I was drawn to the astonishing district and its astonishing inhabitants. The Five Towns, to me, was like the East to those who have smelt the East: it "called."

"I'll tell you what we *could* do," said Mrs. Brindley. "We could put him on to Dr. Stirling."

"So we could!" Brindley agreed. "Wife, this is one of your bright, intelligent days. We'll put you on to the doctor, Loring. I'll impress on him that he must keep you constantly amused till I get back, which I fear it won't be early. This is what we call manners, you know,—to invite a fellow creature to travel a hundred and fifty miles to spend two days here, and then to turn him out before he's been in the house an hour. It's *us*, that is! But the truth of the matter is, the birthday business might be a bit serious. It might easily cost me fifty quid and no end of diplomacy. If you were a married man you'd know that the ten plagues of Egypt are simply nothing in comparison with your wife's relations. And she's over eighty, the old lady."

"I'll give you ten plagues of Egypt!" Mrs. Brindley menaced her spouse, as she wafted the boys from the room. "Mr. Loring, do take some more of that cheese if you fancy it." She vanished.

Within ten minutes Brindley was conducting me to the doctor's, whose house was on the way to the station. In its spacious porch, he explained the circumstances in six words, depositing me like a parcel. The doctor, who had once by mysterious medicaments saved my frail organism from the consequences of one of Brindley's Falstaffian "nights," hospitably protested his readiness to sacrifice patients to my pleasure.

"It'll be a chance for MacIlroy," said he.

"Who's MacIlroy?" I asked.

"MacIlroy is another Scotchman," growled Brindley. "Extraordinary how they stick together! When he wanted an assistant, do you suppose he looked about for some one in the district, some one who understood us and loved us and could take a hand at bridge? Not he! Off he goes to Cupar, or somewhere, and comes back with another stage Scotchman, named MacIlroy. Now listen here, Doc! A charge to keep you have, and mind you keep it, or I'll never pay your confounded bill. We'll knock on the window to-night as we come back. In the meantime you can show Loring your etchings, and pray for me." And to me: "Here's a latchkey." With no further ceremony, he hurried away to join his wife and children at Bleakridge Station. In such singular manner was I transferred forcibly from host to host.

Chapter II

The doctor and I resembled each other in this: that there was no offensive affability about either of us. Tho abounding in good nature, we could not be-

come intimate by a sudden act of volition. Our conversation was difficult, unnatural, and by gusts falsely
familiar. He displayed to me his bachelor house, his
etchings, a few specimens of modern *rouge flambé* ware
made at Knype, his whisky, his celebrated prize-win-
ning fox-terrier Titus, the largest collection of books
in the Five Towns, and photographs of Marischal College, Aberdeen. Then we fell flat, socially prone. Sitting in his study, with Titus between us on the hearth-
rug, we knew no more what to say or do. I regretted
that Brindley's wife's grandmother should have been
born on a fifteenth of February. Brindley was a viva-
cious talker, he could be trusted to talk. I, too, am a
good talker—with another good talker. With a bad
talker I am just a little worse than he is. The doctor
said abruptly after a nerve-trying silence that he had
forgotten a most important call at Hanbridge, and
would I care to go with him in the car? I was and
still am convinced that he was simply inventing. He
wanted to break the sinister spell by getting out of the
house, and he had not the face to suggest a sortie into
the streets of the Five Towns as a promenade of
pleasure.

So we went forth, splashing warily through the rich
mud and the dank mist of Trafalgar Road, past all
those strange little Indian-red houses, and ragged empty
spaces, and poster-hoardings, and rounded kilns, and
high smoking chimneys, up-hill, down-hill, and up-hill
again, encountering and overtaking many electric trams
that dipped and rose like ships at sea, into Crown
Square, the centre of Hanbridge, the metropolis of the
Five Towns. And while the doctor paid his mysterious
call, I stared around me at the large shops and the
banks and the gilded hotels. Down the radiating

street-vistas I could make out the façades of halls, theaters, chapels. Trams rumbled continually in and out of the square. They seemed to enter casually, to hesitate a few moments as if at a loss, and then to decide with a nonchalant clang of bells that they might as well go off somewhere else in search of something more interesting. They were rather like human beings who are condemned to live for ever in a place of which they are sick beyond the expressiveness of words.

And indeed the influence of Crown Square, with its large effects of terra cotta, plate glass, and gold letters, all under a heavy skyscape of drab smoke, was depressing. A few very seedy men (sharply contrasting with the fine delicacy of costly things behind plate-glass) stood doggedly here and there in the mud, immobilized by the gloomy enchantment of the square. Two of them turned to look at Stirling's motor-car and me. They gazed fixedly for a long time, and then one said, only his lips moving:

"Has Tommy stood thee that there quart o' beer as he promised thee?"

No reply, no response of any sort, for a further long period! Then the other said, with grim resignation:

"Ay!"

The conversation ceased, having made a little oasis in the dismal desert of their silent scrutiny of the car. Except for an occasional stamp of the foot they never moved. They just doggedly and indifferently stood, blown upon by all the nipping drafts of the square, and as it might be sinking deeper and deeper into its dejection. As for me, instead of desolating, the harsh disconsolateness of the scene seemed to uplift me; I savored it with joy, as one savors the melancholy of a tragic work of art.

"We might go down to the *Signal* offices, and worry Buchanan a bit," said the doctor cheerfully when he came back to the car. This was the second of his inspirations.

Buchanan, of whom I had heard, was another Scotchman and the editor of the sole daily organ of the Five Towns, an evening newspaper cried all day in the streets and read by the entire population. Its green sheet appeared to be a permanent waving feature of the main thoroughfares. The offices lay round a corner close by, and as we drew up in front of them a crowd of tattered urchins interrupted their diversions in the sodden road to celebrate our glorious arrival by unanimously yelling at the top of their strident and hoarse voices:

"Hooray! Hoo—bl—dy—ray!"

Abashed, I followed my doctor into the shelter of the building, a new edifice, capacious and considerable, but horribly faced with terra cotta, and quite unimposing, lacking in the spectacular effect; like nearly everything in the Five Towns, carelessly and scornfully ugly! The mean, swinging double-doors returned to the assault when you pushed them, and hit you viciously. In a dark, countered room marked "Enquiries" there was nobody.

"Hi, there!" called the doctor.

A head appeared at a door.

"Mr. Buchanan upstairs?"

"Yes," snapped the head, and disappeared.

Up a dark staircase we went, and at the summit were half flung back again by another self-acting door.

In the room to which we next came an old man and a youngish one were bent over a large, littered table, scribbling on and arranging pieces of gray tissue paper and telegrams. Behind the old man stood a boy. Neither of them looked up.

"Mr. Buchanan in his——" the doctor began to question. "Oh! There you are!"

The editor was standing in hat and muffler at the window, gazing out. His age was about that of the doctor, forty or so; and like the doctor he was rather stout and clean-shaven. Their Scotch accents mingled in greeting, the doctor's being the more marked. Buchanan shook my hand with a certain courtliness, indicating that he was well accustomed to receive strangers. As an expert in small talk, however, he shone no brighter than his visitors, and the three of us stood there by the window awkwardly, in the heaped disorder of the room, while the other two men scratched and fidgeted with bits of paper at the soiled table.

Suddenly and savagely the old man turned on the boy:

"What the hades are you waiting there for?"

"I thought there was something else, sir."

"Sling your hook."

Buchanan winked at Stirling and me as the boy slouched off and the old man blandly resumed his writing.

"Perhaps you'd like to look over the place?" Buchanan suggested politely to me. "I'll come with you. It's all I'm fit for to-day. . . . 'Flu!" He glanced at Stirling, and yawned.

"Ye ought to be in bed," said Stirling.

"Yes. I know. I've known it for twelve years. I shall go to bed as soon as I get a bit of time to myself. Well, will you come? The half-time results are beginning to come in."

A telephone-bell rang impatiently.

"You might just see what that is, boss," said the old man without looking up.

Buchanan went to the telephone and replied into it: "Yes? What? Oh! Myatt? Yes, he's playing. . . . Of course I'm sure! Good-bye." He turned to the old man: "It's another of 'em wanting to know if Myatt is playing. Birmingham, this time."

"Ah!" exclaimed the old man, still writing.

"It's because of the betting," Buchanan glanced at me. "The odds are on Knype now,—three to two."

"If Myatt is playing, Knype have got me to thank for it," said the doctor, surprisingly.

"You?"

"Me! He fetched me to his wife this morning. She's nearing her confinement. False alarm. I guaranteed him at least another twelve hours."

"Oh! So that's it, is it?" Buchanan murmured.

Both the sub-editors raised their heads.

"That's it," said the doctor.

"Some people were saying he'd quarrelled with the trainer again, and was shamming," said Buchanan. "But I didn't believe that. There's no hanky-panky about Jos Myatt, anyhow."

I learnt in answer to my questions that a great and terrible football match was at that moment in progress at Knype, a couple of miles away, between the Knype Club and the Manchester Rovers. It was conveyed to me that the importance of this match was almost national, and that the entire district was practically holding its breath till the result should be known. The half-time result was one goal each.

"If Knype lose," said Buchanan explanatorily, "they'll find themselves pushed out of the First League at the end of the season. That's a cert . . . one of the

oldest clubs in England! Semi-finalists for the E
Cup in '78."

" '79," corrected the elder sub-editor.

I gathered that the crisis was grave.

"And Myatt's the captain, I suppose?" said I.

"No. But he's the finest full-back in the League."

I then had a vision of Myatt as a great man. By
an effort of the imagination I perceived that the
equivalent of the fate of nations depended upon him.
I recollected, now, large yellow posters on the board-
ings we had passed, with the names of Knype and of
Manchester Rovers in letters a foot high and the
legend "League match at Knype" over all. It seemed
to me that the heroic name of Jos Myatt, if truly he
were the finest full-back in the League, if truly his
presence or absence affected the betting as far off as
Birmingham, ought also to have been on the posters,
together with possibly his portrait. I saw Jos Myatt
as a matador, with a long ribbon of scarlet necktie
down his breast, and embroidered trousers.

"Why," said Buchanan, "if Knype drop into the Second Division, they'll never pay another dividend! It'll
be all up with first class football in the Five Towns!"

The interests involved seemed to grow more com-
plicated. And here I had been in the district nearly
four hours without having guessed that the district was
quivering in the tense excitement of gigantic issues!
And here was this Scotch doctor, at whose word the
great Myatt would have declined to play, never saying
a syllable about the affair, until a chance remark from
Buchanan loosened his tongue. But all doctors are
strangely secretive. Secretiveness is one of their chief
private pleasures.

"Come and see the pigeons, eh?" said Buchanan.

igeons!" I repeated.

We give the results of over a hundred matches in
Football Edition," said Buchanan, and added: "not
unting Rugby."

As we left the room two boys dodged round us into
it, bearing telegrams.

In a moment we were, in the most astonishing manner, on a leaden roof of the *Signal* offices. High factory
chimneys rose over the horizon of slates on every side,
blowing thick smoke into the general murk of the
afternoon sky, and crossing the western crimson with
long pennons of black. And out of the murk there
came from afar a blue-and-white pigeon which circled
largely several times over the offices of the *Signal*. At
length it descended, and I could hear the whirr of its
strong wings. The wings ceased to beat and the pigeon
slanted downwards in a curve, its head lower than its
wide tail. Then the little head gradually rose and the
tail fell; the curve had changed, the pace slackened;
the pigeon was calculating with all its brain; eyes,
wings, tail and feet were being coordinated to the resolution of an intricate mechanical problem. The pinkish
claws seemed to grope—and after an instant of hesitation, the thing was done, the problem solved; the
pigeon, with delicious gracefulness, had established
equilibrium on the ridge of a pigeon-cote, and folded
its wings, and was peering about with strange motions
of its extremely movable head. Presently it flew down
to the leads, waddled to and fro with the ungainly
gestures of a fat woman of sixty, and disappeared into
the cote. At the same moment the boy who had been
dismissed from the sub-editor's room ran forward and
entered the cote by a wire-screened door.

"Handy things, pigeons!" said the doctor as we

approached to examine the cote. Fifty or sixty p[
were cooing and strutting in it. There was a pr[
wings as the boy seized the last arriving mess[

"Give it here!" Buchanan ordered.

The boy handed over a thin tube of paper [
had unfastened from the bird's leg. Buchanan [
it and showed it to me. I read: "Midland Fed[
Axe United, Macclesfield Town. Match aba[
after half-hour's play owing to fog. Three fort[

"Three forty-five," said Buchanan, looking [
watch. "He's done the ten miles in half a [
roughly. Not bad. First time we tried pige[
as far off as Axe. Here, boy!" And he rest[
paper to the boy, who gave it to another l[
departed with it.

"Man," said the doctor, eyeing Buchanan. "[
business out here. Ye're not precisely a pigeon. [

Down we went, one after another, by the ladd[
now we fell into the composing-room, where Buch[
said he felt warmer. An immense, dirty, white-was[
apartment crowded with linotypes and other machines,
in front of which sat men in white aprons, tapping,
tapping,—gazing at documents pinned at the level of
their eyes,—and tapping, tapping. A kind of cavernous
retreat in which monstrous iron growths rose out of the
floor and were met half way by electric flowers that
had their roots in the ceiling! In this jungle there was
scarcely room for us to walk. Buchanan explained the
linotypes to me. I watched, as tho romantically
dreaming, the flashing descent of letter after letter, a
rain of letters into the belly of the machine; then,
going round to the back, I watched the same letters
rising again in a close, slow procession and sorting
themselves by themselves at the top in readiness to

again to the tapping, tapping of a man in a
te apron. And while I was watching all that,
omehow, by a faculty which we have, at the
see pigeons far overhead, arriving and arriv-
the murk from beyond the verge of chimneys.
ious, isn't it?" said Stirling.

imagine that he had not the faculty by which
he pigeons.

erend, bearded, spectacled man, with his shirt-
rolled up and an apron stretched over his
rical paunch, strolled slowly along an alley,
at a galley-proof with an ingenious air just
ad never seen a galley-proof before.

stick more than a column already," said he
ally, offering the long paper, and then gravely
at Buchanan, with head bent forward, not
his spectacles but over them.

editor negligently accepted the proof, and I read
ies of titles: "Knype v. Manchester Rovers.
ord Gate. Fifteen thousand spectators. Two goals
n twelve minutes. Myatt in form. Special Report."
Buchanan gave the slip back without a word.

"There you are!" said he to me, as another com-
positor near us attached a piece of tissue paper to his
machine. It was the very paper that I had seen come
out of the sky, but its contents had been enlarged and
amended by the sub-editorial pen. The man began
tapping, tapping, and the letters began to flash downwards on their way to tell a quarter of a million people
that Axe v. Macclesfield had been stopped by fog.

"I suppose that Knype match is over by now?" I
said.

"Oh, no!" said Buchanan. "The second half has
scarcely begun."

"Like to go?" Stirling asked.

"Well," I said, feeling adventurous, "it's a notion, isn't it?"

"You can run Mr. Loring down there in five or six minutes," said Buchanan. "And he's probably never seen anything like it before. You might call here as you come home, and see the paper on the machines."

Chapter III

We were on the Grand Stand, which was packed with men whose eyes were fixed, with an unconscious but intense effort, on a common object. Among the men were a few women in furs and wraps, equally absorbed. Nobody took any notice of us as we insinuated our way up a rickety flight of wooden stairs, but when by misadventure we grazed a human being the elbow of that being shoved itself automatically and fiercely outwards, to repel. I had an impression of hats, caps, and woolly overcoats stretched in long parallel lines, and of grimy raw planks everywhere presenting possibly dangerous splinters, save where use had worn them into smooth shininess. Then gradually I became aware of the vast field, which was more brown then green. Around the field was a wide border of infinitesimal hats and pale faces, rising in tiers, and beyond this border fences, hoardings, chimneys, furnaces, gasometers, telegraph-poles, houses, and dead trees. And here and there, perched in strange perilous places, even high up towards the somber sky, were more human beings clinging. On the field itself, at one end of it, were a scattered handful of doll-like figures, motionless; some had white bodies, others red; and three were in black:

all were so small and so far off that they seemed to be
mere unimportant casual incidents in whatever recondite affair it was that was proceeding. Then a whistle
shrieked, and all these figures began simultaneously to
move, and then I saw a ball in the air. An obscure,
uneasy murmuring rose from the immense multitude
like an invisible but audible vapor. The next instant
the vapor had condensd into a suddn shout. Now I
saw the ball rolling solitary in the middle of the field,
and a single red doll racing towards it; at one end was
a confused group of red and white, and at the other
two white dolls, rather lonely in the expanse. The
single red doll overtook the ball and scudded along
with it at his twinkling toes. A great voice behind
me bellowed with an incredible volume of sound:

"Now Jos!"

And another voice, further away, bellowed:

"Now Jos!"

And still more distantly the grim warning shot forth
from the crowd:

"Now Jos! Now Jos!"

The nearer of the white dolls, as the red one approached, sprang forward. I could see a leg. And the
ball was flying back in a magnificent curve into the
skies; it passed out of my sight, and then I heard a
bump on the slates of the roof of the grand stand, and
it fell among the crowd in the stand-enclosure. But
almost before the flight of the ball had commenced, a
terrific roar of relief had rolled formidably round the
field, and out of that roar, like rockets out of thick
smoke, burst acutely ecstatic cries of adoration:

"Bravo Jos!"

"Good old Jos!"

The leg had evidently been Jos's leg. The nearer of

these two white dolls must be Jos, darling of fifteen thousand frenzied people.

Stirling punched a neighbor in the side to attract his attention.

"What's the score?" he demanded of the neighbor, who scowled and then grinned.

"Two—one—agen uz!" The other growled. "It'll take our b——s all their time to draw. They're playing a man short."

"Accident?"

"No! Referee ordered him off for rough play."

Several spectators began to explain, passionately, furiously, that the referee's action was utterly bereft of common sense and justice; and I gathered that a less gentlemanly crowd would undoubtedly have lynched the referee. The explanations died down, and everybody except me resumed his fierce watch on the field.

I was recalled from the exercise of a vague curiosity upon the set, anxious faces around me by a crashing, whooping cheer which in volume and sincerity of joy surpassed all noises in my experience. This massive cheer reverberated round the field like the echoes of a battleship's broadside in a fiord. But it was human, and therefore more terrible than guns. I instinctively thought: "If such are the symptoms of pleasure, what must be the symptoms of pain or 'isappointment?" Simultaneously with the expulsion of the unique noise the expression of the faces changed. Eyes sparkled; teeth became prominent in enormous, uncontrolled smiles. Ferocious satisfaction had to find vent in ferocious gestures, wreaked either upon dead wood or upon the living tissues of fellow creatures. The gentle, mannerly sound of hand-clapping was a kind of light froth on the surface of the billowy sea of heart-felt applause. The host of the fifteen thousand might have just had their lives saved, or their children snatched from destruction and their wives from dishonor; they might have been preserved from bankruptcy, starvation, prison, torture; they might have been rewarding with their impassioned worship a band of national heroes. But it was not so. All that had happened was that the ball had rolled into the net of the Manchester Rovers' goal. Knype had drawn level. The reputation of the Five Towns before the jury of expert opinion that could distinguish between first-class football and second-class was maintained intact. I could hear specialists around me proving that tho Knype had yet five League matches to play, its situation was safe. They pointed excitedly to a huge boarding at one end of the ground on which appeared names of other clubs with changing figures. These clubs included the clubs which Knype would have to meet before the end of the season, and the figures indicated their fortunes on various grounds similar to this ground all over the country. If a goal was scored in Newcastle or in Southampton, the very Peru of first-class football, it was registered on that board and its possible effect on the destinies of Knype was instantly assessed. The calculations made were dizzying.

Then a little flock of pigeons flew up and separated, under the illusion that they were free agents and masters of the air, but really wafted away to fixed destinations on the stupendous atmospheric waves of still-continued cheering.

After a minute or two the ball was restarted, and the greater noise had diminished to the sensitive uneasy murmur which responded like a delicate instrument to the fluctuations of the game. Each feat and maneuver of Knype drew generous applause in proportion to its intention or its success, and each sleight of the Manchester Rovers, successful or not, provoked a holy disgust. The attitude of the host had passed beyond morality into religion.

Then, again, while my attention had lapsed from the field, a devilish, a barbaric, and a deafening yell broke from those fifteen thousand passionate hearts. It thrilled me; it genuinely frightened me. I involuntarily made the motion of swallowing. After the thunderous crash of anger from the host came the thin sound of a whistle. The game stopped. I heard the same word repeated again and again, in divers tones of exasperated fury:

"Foul!"

I felt that I was hemmed in by potential homicides, whose arms were lifted in the desire of murder and whose features were changed from the likeness of man into the corporeal form of some pure and terrible instinct.

And I saw a long doll rise from the ground and approach a lesser doll with threatening hands.

"Foul! Foul!"

"Go it, Jos! Knock his neck out! Jos! He tripped thee up!"

There was a prolonged gesticulatory altercation between the three black dolls in leathern leggings and several of the white and the red dolls. At last one of the mannikins in leggings shrugged his shoulders, made a definite gesture to the other two, and walked away towards the edge of the field nearest the stand. It was the unprincipled referee; he had disallowed the foul. In the protracted duel between the offending Manchester forward and the great, honest Jos Myatt he

had given another point to the enemy. As soon as the
host realized the infamy, it yelled once more in height-
ened fury. It seemed to surge in masses against the
thick iron railings that alone stood between the referee
and death. The discreet referee was approaching the
grand stand as the least unsafe place. In a second a
handful of executioners had somehow got on to the
grass. And in the next second several policemen were
in front of them, not striking nor striving to intimidate,
but heavily pushing them into bounds.

"Get back there!" cried a few abrupt, commanding
voices from the stand.

The referee stood with his hands in his pockets and
his whistle in his mouth. I think that in that moment
of acutest suspense the whole of his earthly career must
have flashed before him in fantasmagoria. And then
the crisis was past. The inherent gentlemanliness of
the outraged host had triumphed and the referee was
spared.

"Served him right if they'd man-handled him!" said
a spectator.

"Ay!" said another, gloomily, "Ay! And th' Football Association 'ud ha' fined us maybe a hundred quid
and disqualified th' ground for the rest o' th' season!"

"D—n th' Football Association!"

"Ay! But you canna'!"

"Now lads! Play up Knype! Now lads! Give 'em
hot hell!" Different voices heartily encouraged the
home team as the ball was thrown into play.

The fouling Manchester forward immediately resumed possession of the ball. Experience could not
teach him. He parted with the ball and got it again,
twice. The devil was in him and in the ball. The
devil was driving him towards Myatt. They met. And

then came a sound quite new: a cracking sound, somewhat like the snapping of a bough, but sharper, more decisive.

"By Jove!" exclaimed Stirling. "That's his bone!"

And instantly he was off down the staircase and I after him. But he was not the first doctor on the field. Nothing had been unforeseen in the wonderful organization of this enterprise. A pigeon sped away and an official doctor and an official stretcher appeared, miraculously, simultaneously. It was tremendous. It inspired awe in me.

"He asked for it!" I heard a man say as I hesitated on the shore of the ocean of mud.

Then I knew that it was Manchester and not Knype that had suffered. The confusion and hubbub were in a high degree disturbing and puzzling. But one emotion emerged clear: pleasure. I felt it myself. I was aware of joy in that the two sides were now levelled to ten men apiece. I was mystically identified with the Five Towns, absorbed into their life. I could discern on every face the conviction that a divine providence was in this affair, that God could not be mocked. I too had this conviction. I could discern also on every face the fear lest the referee might give a foul against the hero Myatt, or even order him off the field, tho of course the fracture was a simple accident. I too had this fear. It was soon dispelled by the news which swept across the entire enclosure like a sweet smell, that the referee had adopted the theory of a simple accident. I saw vaguely policemen, a stretcher, streaming crowds, and my ears heard a monstrous universal babbling. And then the figure of Stirling detached itself from the moving disorder and came to me.

"Well, Myatt's calf was harder than the other chap's, that's all," he said.

"Which *is* Myatt?" I asked, for the red and the white dolls had all vanished at close quarters, and were replaced by unrecognizably gigantic human animals, still clad, however, in dolls' vests and dolls' knickerbockers.

Stirling warningly jerked his head to indicate a man not ten feet away from me. This was Myatt, the hero of the host and the darling of populations. I gazed up at him. His mouth and his left knee were red with blood, and he was piebald with thick patches of mud from his tousled crown to his enormous boot. His blue eyes had a heavy, stupid, honest glance; and of the three qualities stupidity predominated. He seemed to be all feet, knees, hands, and elbows. His head was very small,—the sole remainder of the doll in him.

A little man approached him, conscious—somewhat too obviously conscious—of his right to approach. Myatt nodded.

"Ye'n settled *him,* seemingly, Jos!" said the little man.

"Well," said Myatt, with slow bitterness. "Hadn't he been blooming well begging and praying for it, aw afternoon. Hadn't he now?"

The little man nodded. Then he said in a lower tone:

"How's missis, like?"

"Her's altogether yet," said Myatt. "Or I'd none ha' played!"

"I've bet Watty half-a-dollar as it inna' a lad!" said the little man.

Myatt seemed angry.

"Wilt bet me half a *quid* as it inna' a lad?" he de-

manded, bending down and scowling and sticking out
his muddy chin.

"Ay!" said the little man, not blenching.

"Evens?"

"Evens."

"I'll take thee, Charlie," said Myatt, resuming his
calm.

The whistle sounded. And several orders were given
to clear the field. Eight minutes had been lost over a
broken leg, but Stirling said that the referee would
surely deduct them from the official time, so that after
all the game would not be shortened.

"I'll be up yon, to-morra morning," said the little
man.

Myatt nodded and departed. Charlie, the little man,
turned on his heel and proudly rejoined the crowd. He
had been seen of all in converse with supreme greatness.

Stirling and I also retired; and tho Jos Myatt had
not even done his doctor the honor of seeing him,
neither of us, I think, was quite without a consciousness of glory: I cannot imagine why. The rest of the
game was flat and tame. Nothing occurred. The
match ended in a draw.

Chapter IV

We were swept from the Football ground on a furious flood of humanity,—carried forth and flung down
a slope into a large waste space that separated the
ground from the nearest streets of little reddish houses.
At the bottom of the slope, on my suggestion, we halted
for a few moments aside, while the current rushed forward and, spreading out, inundated the whole space in
one marvellous minute. The impression of the multi-

tude streaming from that gap in the wooden wall was
like nothing more than the impression of a burst main
which only the emptying of the reservoir will assuage.
Anybody who wanted to commit suicide might have
stood in front of that gap and had his wish. He would
not have been noticed. The interminable and implacable infantry charge would have passed unheedingly
over him. A silent, pre-occupied host, bent on something else now, and perhaps teased by the inconvenient
thought that after all a draw is not as good as a win!
It hurried blindly, instinctively outwards, knees and
chins protruding, hands deep in pockets, chilled feet
stamping. Occasionally some one stopped or slackened
to light a pipe, and on being curtly bunted by a blind
force from behind, accepted the hint as an atom accepts
the law of gravity. The fever and ecstasy were over.
What fascinated the Southern in me was the grim
taciturnity, the steady stare (vacant or dreaming), and
the heavy, muffled, multitudinous tramp shaking the
cindery earth. The flood continued to rage through
the gap.

Our automobile had been left at the Haycock Hotel;
we went to get it, braving the inundation. Nearly
opposite the stableyard the electric trams started for
Hanbridge, Bursley and Turnhill, and for Longshaw.
Here the crowd was less dangerous, but still very
formidable—to my eyes. Each tram as it came up,
was savagely assaulted, seized, crammed, and possessed,
with astounding rapidity. Its steps were the western
bank of a Beresina. At a given moment the inured
conductor, brandishing his leather-shielded arm with a
pitiless gesture, thrust aspirants down into the mud and
the tram rolled powerfully away. All this in silence.

After a few minutes a bicyclist swished along through

the mud, taking the far side of the road, which was comparatively free. He wore gray trousers, heavy boots, and a dark cut-away coat, up the back of which a line of caked mud had deposited itself. On his head was a bowler-hat.

"How do, Jos?" cried a couple of boys, cheekily. And then there were a few adult greetings of respect It was the hero, in haste.

"Out of it, there!" he warned impeders, between his teeth, and plugged on with bent head.

"He keeps the Foaming Quart up at Toft End," said the doctor. "It's the highest pub in the Five Towns. He used to be what they call a pot-hunter, a racing bicyclist, you know. But he's got past that, and he'll soon be past football. He's thirty-four if he's a day. That's one reason why he's so independent—that and because he's almost the only genuine native in the team."

"Why?" I asked. "Where do they come from, then?"

"Oh!" said Stirling as he gently started the car. "The club buys 'em, up and down the country. Four of 'em are Scots. A few years ago, an Oldham Club offered Knype £500 for Myatt, a big price—more than he's worth now! But he wouldn't go, tho they guaranteed to put him into a first-class pub—a free house. He's never cost Knype anything except his wages and the good-will of the Foaming Quart."

"What are his wages?"

"Don't know exactly. Not much. The Football Association fix a maximum. I daresay about four pounds a week. *Hi there! Are you deaf?*"

"Thee mind what tha'rt about!" responded a stout loiterer in our path, "or I'll take thy ears home for my tea, mester."

Stirling laughed.

In a few minutes we had arrived at Hanbridge, splashing all the way between two processions that crowded either footpath. And in the middle of the road was a third procession, of trams,—tram following tram, each gorged with passengers, frothing at the step with passengers; not the lackadaisical trams that I had seen earlier in the afternoon in Crown Square; a different race of trams, eager and impetuous velocities. We reached the *Signal* offices. No crowd of urchins to salute us this time!

Under the earth was the machine-room of the *Signal*. It reminded me of the bowels of a ship, so full was it of machinery. One huge machine clattered slowly, and a folded green thing dropped strangely on to a little iron table in front of us. Buchanan opened it, and I saw that the broken leg was in it at length, together with a statement that in the *Signal's* opinion the sympathy of every true sportsman would be with the disabled player. I began to say something to Buchanan, when suddenly I could not hear my own voice. The great machine, with another behind us, was working at a fabulous speed and with a fabulous clatter. All that my startled senses could clearly disentangle was that the blue arc-lights above us blinked occasionally, and that folded green papers were snowing down upon the iron table far faster than the eye could follow them. Tall lads in aprons elbowed me away and carried off the green papers in bundles, but not more quickly than the machine shed them. Buchanan put his lips to my ear. But I could hear nothing. I shook my head. He smiled, and led us out from the tumult.

"Come and see the boys take them," he said at the foot of the stairs.

In a sort of hall on the ground floor was a long
counter, and beyond the counter a system of steel railings in parallel lines, so arranged that a person entering
at the public door could only reach the counter by
passing up or down each alley in succession. These
steel lanes, which absolutely ensured the triumph of
right over might, were packed with boys—the ragged
urchins whom we had seen playing in the street. But
not urchins now; rather young tigers! Perhaps half a
dozen had reached the counter; the rest were massed
behind, shouting and quarrelling. Through a hole in
the wall, at the level of the counter, bundles of papers
shot continuously, and were snatched up by servers,
who distributed them in smaller bundles to the hungry
boys; who flung down metal discs in exchange and fled,
fled madly as tho fiends were after them, through a
third door, out of the pandemonium into the darkling
street. And unceasingly the green papers appeared at
the hole in the wall and unceasingly they were plucked
away and borne off by those maddened children, whose
destination was apparently Aix or Ghent, and whose
wings were their tatters.

"What are those discs?" I enquired.

"The lads have to come and buy them earlier in the
day," said Buchanan. "We haven't time to sell this
edition for cash, you see."

"Well," I said as we left, "I'm very much obliged."

"What on earth for?" Buchanan asked.

"Everything," I said.

We returned through the squares of Hanbridge and
by Trafalgar Road to Stirling's house at Bleakridge.
And everywhere in the deepening twilight I could see
the urchins, often hatless and sometimes scarcely shod,
scudding over the lamp-reflecting mire with sheets of

wavy green, and above the noises of traffic I could hear the shrill outcry: "*Signal*. Football Edition. Football edition. *Signal*." The world was being informed of the might of Jos Myatt, and of the averting of disaster from Knype, and of the results of over a hundred other matches—not counting Rugby.

Chapter V

During the course of the evening, when Stirling had thoroughly accustomed himself to the state of being in sole charge of an expert from the British Museum, London, and the high walls round his more private soul had yielded to my timid but constant attacks, we grew fairly intimate. And in particular the doctor proved to me that his reputation for persuasive raciness with patients was well founded. Yet up to the time of desert I might have been justified in supposing that that much praised "manner" in a sick-room was nothing but a provincial legend. Such may be the influence of a quite inoffensive and shy Londoner in the country. At half-past ten, Titus being already asleep for the night in an armchair, we sat at ease over the fire in the study telling each other stories. We had dealt with the arts, and with medicine; now we were dealing with life, in those aspects of it which cause men to laugh and women uneasily to wonder. Once or twice we had mentioned the Brindleys. The hour for their arrival was come. But being deeply comfortable and content where I was, I felt no impatience. Then there was a tap on the window.

"That's Bobbie!" said Stirling, rising slowly from his chair. "*He* won't refuse whisky, even if you do. I'd better get another bottle."

The tap was repeated, peevishly.

"I'm coming, laddie!" Stirling protested.

He slippered out through the hall and through the surgery to the side door, I following, and Titus sneezing and snuffling in the rear.

"I say, mester," said a heavy voice as the doctor opened the door. It was not Brindley, but Jos Myatt. Unable to locate the bell-push in the dark, he had characteristically attacked the sole illuminated window. He demanded, or he commanded, very curtly, that the doctor should go up instantly to the Foaming Quart at Toft End.

Stirling hesitated a moment.

"All right, my man," said he calmly.

"Now?" the heavy, suspicious voice on the doorstep insisted.

"I'll be there before ye if ye don't sprint, man. I'll run up in the car." Stirling shut the door. I heard footsteps on the gravel path outside.

"Ye heard?" said he to me. "And what am I to do with ye?"

"I'll go with you, of course," I answered.

"I may be kept up there a while."

"I don't care," I said roisterously. "It's a pub and I'm a traveller."

Stirling's household was in bed, and his assistant gone home. While he and Titus got out the car, I wrote a line for the Brindleys: "Gone with doctor to see patient at Toft End. Don't wait up. A. L." This we pushed under Brindley's front door on our way forth. Very soon we were vibrating up a steep street on the first speed of the car, and the yellow reflection of distant furnaces began to shine over house roofs below us. It was exhilaratingly cold, a clear and frosty night, tonic,

bracing after the enclosed warmth of the study. I was
joyous, but silently. We had quitted the kingdom of
the god Pan; we were in Lucina's realm, its consequence, where there is no laughter. We were on a
mission.

"I didn't expect this," said Stirling.

"No?" I said. "But seeing that he fetched you this
morning——"

"Oh! That was only in order to be sure, for himself.
His sister was there, in charge. Seemed very capable.
Knew all about everything. Until ye get to the high
social status of a clerk or a draper's assistant, people
seem to manage to have their children without professional assistance."

"Then do you think there's anything wrong?" I
asked.

"I'd not be surprized."

He changed to the second speed as the car topped the
first bluff. We said no more. The night and the mission solemnized us. And gradually, as we rose towards
the purple skies, the Five Towns wrote themselves out
in fire on the irregular plain below.

"That's Hanbridge Town Hall," said Stirling, pointing to the right. "And that's Bursley Town Hall," he
said, pointing to the left. And there were many other
beacons, dominating the jewelled street-lines that faded
on the horizon into golden-tinted smoke.

The road was never quite free of houses. After
occurring but sparsely for half a mile, they thickened
into a village—the suburb of Bursley called Toft End.
I saw a moving red light in front of us. It was the
reverse of Myatt's bicycle lantern. The car stopped
near the dark façade of the inn, of which two yellow
windows gleamed. Stirling, under Myatt's shouted

guidance, backed into an obscure yard under cover. The engine ceased to throb.

"Friend of mine," he introduced me to Myatt. "By the way, Loring, pass me my bag, will you? Mustn't forget that." Then he extinguished the acetylene lamps, and there was no light in the yard except the ray of the bicycle lantern which Myatt held in his hand. We groped towards the house. Strange, every step that I take in the Five Towns seems to have the genuine quality of an adventure!

Chapter VI

In five minutes I was of no account in the scheme of things at Toft End, and I began to wonder why I had come. Stirling, my sole protector, had vanished up the dark stairs of the house, following a stout, youngish wom·n in a white apron, who bore a candle. Jos Myatt, behind, said to me: "Happen you'd better go in there, mester," pointing to a half open door at the foot of the stairs. I went into a little room at the rear of the bar-parlor. A good fire burned in a small old-fashioned grate, but there was no other light. The inn was closed to customers, it being past eleven o'clock. On a bare table I perceived a candle, and ventured to put a match to it. I then saw almost exactly such a room as one would expect to find at the rear of the bar-parlor of an inn on the outskirts of an industrial town. It appeared to serve the double purpose of a living-room and of a retreat for favored customers. The table was evidently one at which men drank. On a shelf was a row of bottles, more or less empty, bearing names famous in newspaper advertisements and in the House of Lords. The dozen chairs suggested an

acute bodily discomfort such as would only be toler-
ated by a sitter all of whose sensory faculties were
centered in his palace. On a broken chair in a corner
was an insecure pile of books. A smaller table was
covered with a checkered cloth on which were a few
plates. Along one wall, under the window, ran a pitch-
pine sofa upholstered with a stuff slightly dissimilar
from that on the table. The mattress of the sofa was
uneven and its surface wrinkled, and old newspapers
and pieces of brown paper had been stowed away between it and the framework. The chief article of furniture was an effective walnut bookcase, the glass-doors
of which were curtained with red cloth. The window,
wider than it was high, was also curtained with red
cloth. The walls, papered in a saffron tint, bore framed
advertisements and a few photographs of self-conscious
persons. The ceiling was as obscure as heaven; the
floor tiled, with a list rug in front of the steel fender.
I put my overcoat on the sofa, picked up the candle
and glanced at the books in the corner: Lavater's in-
destructible work, a paper-covered Whitaker, the
Licensed Victualler's Almanac, "Johnny Ludlow," the
illustrated catalogue of the Exhibition of 1856, Cruden's
Concordance, and seven or eight volumes of Knight's
Penny Encyclopedia. While I was poring on these
titles I heard movements overhead—previously there
had been no sound whatever—and with guilty haste I
restored the candle to the table and placed myself
negligently in front of the fire.
"Now don't let me see ye up here any more till I
fetch ye!" said a woman's distant voice—not crossly,
but firmly. And then, crossly: "Be off with ye now!"
Reluctant boots on the stairs! Jos Myatt entered
to me. He did not speak at first; nor did I. He

avoided my glance. He was still wearing the cutaway
coat with the line of mud up the back. I took out my
watch, not for the sake of information, but from mere
nervousness, and the sight of the watch reminded me
that it would be prudent to wind it up.

"Better not forget that," I said, winding it.

"Ay!" said he gloomily. "It's a tip." And he wound
up his watch; a large, thick, golden one.

This watch-winding established a basis of intercourse
between us.

"I hope everything is going on all right," I murmured.

"What dun ye say?" he asked.

"I say I hope everything is going on all right," I
repeated louder, and jerked my head in the direction
of the stairs, to indicate the place from which he had
come.

"Oh!" he exclaimed, as if surprised. "Now what'll
ye have, mester?" He stood waiting. "It's my call,
to-night."

I explained to him that I never took alcohol. It
was not quite true, but it was as true as most general
propositions are.

"Neither me!" he said shortly, after a pause.

"You're a teetotaler too?" I showed a little involuntary astonishment.

He put forward his chin.

"What do *you* think?" he said confidentially and
scornfully. It was precisely as if he had said: "Do
you think that anybody but a born ass would *not* be a
teetotaler, in my position?"

I sat down on a chair.

"Take th' squab, mester," he said, pointing to the
sofa. I took it.

He picked up the candle; then dropped it, and lighted a lamp which was on the mantelpiece between his vases of blue glass. His movements were very slow, hesitating, and clumsy. Blowing out the candle, which smoked for a long time, he went with the lamp to the bookcase. As the key of the bookcase was in his right pocket and the lamp in his right hand he had to change the lamp, cautiously, from hand to hand. When he opened the cupboard I saw a rich gleam of silver from every shelf of it except the lowest, and I could distinguish the forms of ceremonious cups with pedestals and immense handles.

"I suppose these are your pots?" I said.

"Ay!"

He displayed to me the fruits of his manifold victories. I could see him straining along endless cinder-paths and high-roads under hot suns, his great knees going up and down like treadles amid the plaudits and howls of vast populations. And all that now remained of that glory were these debased and vicious shapes, magnificently useless, grossly ugly, with their inscriptions lost in a mess of flourishes.

"Ay!" he said again, when I had fingered the last of them.

"A very fine show indeed!" I said, resuming the sofa.

He took a penny bottle of ink and a pen out of the bookcase, and also, from the lowest shelf, a bag of money and a long narrow account book. Then he sat down at the table and commenced accountancy. It was clear that he regarded his task as formidable and complex. To see him reckoning the coins, manipulating the pen, splashing the ink, scratching the page; to hear him whispering consecutive numbers aloud, and muttering mysterious anathemas against the untamable

naughtiness of figures,—all this was painful, and with
the painfulness of a simple exercise rendered difficult
by inaptitude and incompetence. I wanted to jump up
and cry to him: "Get out of the way, man, and let me
do it for you! I can do it all while you are wiping
hairs from your pen on your sleeve." I was sorry for
him because he was ridiculous—and even more gro-
tesque than ridiculous. I felt, quite acutely, that it
was a shame that he could not be for ever the central
figure of a field of mud, kicking a ball into long and
grandiose parabolas higher than gasometers, or breaking an occasional leg, surrounded by the violent affection of hearts whose melting-point was the exclamation,
"Good old Jos!" I felt that if he must repose his
existence ought to have been so contrived that he could
repose in impassive and senseless dignity, like a mountain watching the flight of time. The conception of
him tracing symbols in a ledger, counting shillings and
sixpences, descending to arithmetic, and suffering those
humiliations which are the invariable preliminaries to
legitimate fatherhood, was shocking to a nice taste for
harmonious fitness. . . . What, this precious and terrific organism, this slave with a specialty—whom distant towns had once been anxious to buy at the pro-
digious figure of five hundred pounds, obliged to sit in
a mean chamber and wait silently while the woman of
his choice encountered the supreme peril! And he
would "soon be past football!" He was "thirty-four
if a day!" It was the verge of senility! He was no
longer worth five hundred pounds. Perhaps even now
this jointed merchandise was only worth two hundred
pounds! And "they"—the shadowy directors, who
could not kick a ball fifty feet and who would probably
turn sick if they broke a leg—"they" paid him four

pounds a week for being the hero of a quarter of a million of people! He was the chief magnet to draw fifteen thousand sixpences and shillings of a Saturday afternoon into a company's cash box, and here he sat splitting his head over fewer sixpences and shillings than would fill a half-pint pot! Jos, you ought in justice to have been José, with a thin red necktie down your breast (instead of a line of mud up your back), and embroidered breeches on those miraculous legs, and an income of a quarter of a million pesetas, and the languishing acquiescence of innumerable mantillas. Every movement you were getting older and stiffer; every moment was bringing nearer the moment when young men would reply curtly to their doddering elders: "Jos Myatt—who was *'e?*"

The putting away of the ledger, the ink, the pen and the money was as exasperating as their taking-out had been. Then Jos, always too large for the room, crossed the tiled floor and mended the fire. A poker was more suited to his capacity than a pen. He glanced about him, uncertain and anxious, and then crept to the door near the foot of the stairs, and listened. There was no sound; and that was curious. The woman who was bringing into the world the hero's child made no cry that reached us below. Once or twice I had heard muffled movements not quite overhead—somewhere above—but naught else. The doctor and Jos's sister seemed to have retired into a sinister and dangerous mystery. I could not dispel from my mind pictures of what they were watching and what they were doing. The vast, cruel, fumbling clumsiness of nature, her lack of majesty in crises that ought to be majestic, her incurable indignity, disgusted me, aroused my disdain. I wanted, as a philosopher of all the cultures, to feel that the present was indeed a majestic crisis, to be so esteemed by a superior man. I could not. Tho the crisis possibly intimidated me somewhat, yet on behalf of Jos Myatt, I was ashamed of it. This may be reprehensible, but it is true.

He sat down by the fire and looked at the fire. I could not attempt to carry on a conversation with him, and to avoid the necessity for any talk at all, I extended myself on the sofa and averted my face, wondering once again why I had accompanied the doctor to Toft End. The doctor was now in another, an inaccessible world. I dozed, and from my doze I was roused by Jos Myatt going to the door on the stairs.

"Jos," said a voice. "It's a girl."

Then a silence.

I admit there was a flutter in my heart. Another soul, another formed and unchangeable temperament, tumbled into the world! Whence? Whither? . . . As for the quality of majesty,—yes, if silver trumpets had announced the advent, instead of a stout, aproned woman, the moment could not have been more majestic in its sadness. I say "sadness": which is the inevitable and sole effect of these eternal and banal questions, "Whence? Whither?"

"Is her bad?" Jos whispered.

"Her's pretty bad," said the voice, but cheerily. "Bring me up another scuttle o' coal."

When he returned to the parlor, after being again dismissed, I said to him:

"Well, I congratulate you."

"I thank ye!" he said, and sat down. Presently I could hear him muttering to himself, mildly: "Hell! Hell! Hell!"

I thought: "Stirling will not be very long now, and

we can depart home." I looked at my watch. It was a quarter to two. But Stirling did not appear, nor was there any message from him or sign. I had to resign myself to the predicament. As a faint chilliness from the window affected my back I drew my overcoat up to my shoulders as a counterpane. Through a gap between the red curtains of the window I could see a star blazing. It passed behind the curtain with disconcerting rapidity. The universe was swinging and whirling as usual.

Chapter VII

Sounds of knocking disturbed me. In the few seconds that elapsed before I could realize just where I was and why I was there, the summoning knocks were repeated. The early sun was shining through the red blind. I sat up and straightened my hair, involuntarily composing my attitude so that nobody who might enter the room should imagine that I had been other than patiently wideawake all night. The second door of the parlor—that leading to the barroom of the Foaming Quart—was open, and I could see the bar itself, with shelves rising behind it and the upright handles of a beer-engine at one end. Some one whom I could not see was evidently unbolting and unlocking the principal entrance to the inn. Then I heard the scraping of a creaky portal on the floor.

"Well, Jos, lad!"

It was the voice of the little man, Charlie, who had spoken with Myatt on the football field.

"Come in quick, Charlie. It's cowd [cold]," said the voice of Jos Myatt gloomily.

"Ay! Cowd it is, lad! It's above three mile as I've

walked, and thou knows it, Jos. Give us a quartern
o' gin."

The door grated again, and a bolt was drawn.

The two men passed together behind the bar, and so
within my vision. Charlie had a gray muffler round
his neck; his hands were far in his pockets and seemed
to be at strain, as tho trying to prevent his upper
and his lower garments from flying apart. Jos Myatt
was extremely dishevelled. In the little man's demeanor towards the big one, there was now none of
the self-conscious pride in the mere fact of acquaintance
that I had noticed on the field. Clearly the two were
intimate friends, perhaps relatives. While Jos was
dispensing the gin, Charlie said in a low tone:

"Well, what luck, Jos?"

This was the first reference, by either of them, to
the crisis.

Jos deliberately finished pouring out the gin. Then
he said:

"There's two on 'em, Charlie."

"Two on 'em? What mean'st tha', lad?"

"I mean as it's twins."

Charlie and I were equally startled.

"Thou never says!" he murmured, incredulous.

"Ay! One o' both sorts," said Jos.

"Thou never says!" Charlie repeated, holding his
glass of gin steady in his hand.

"One come at summat after one o'clock, and th' other
between five and six. I had for fetch old woman
Eardley to help. It were more than a handful for
Susannah and th' doctor."

Astonishing, that I should have slept through these
events!

"How is her?" asked Charley quietly, as it were

casually. I think this appearance of casualness was
caused by the stoic suppression of the symptoms of
anxiety.

"Her's bad," said Jos briefly.

"And I am na' surprised," said Charlie. And he
lifted the glass. "Well—here's luck." He sipped the
gin, savoring it on his tongue like a connoisseur and
gradually making up his mind about its quality. Then
he took another sip.

"Hast seen her?"

"I seed her for a minute, but our Susannah wouldna'
let me stop i' th' room. Her was raving like."

"Missis?"

"Ay!"

"And th' babbies—hast seen *them?*"

"Ay! But I can make nowt out of 'em. Mrs.
Eardley says as her's never seen no finer."

"Doctor gone?"

"That he has na'! He's bin up there all the blessed
night, in his shirt-sleeves. I give him a stiff glass o'
whisky at five o'clock and that's all as he's had."

Charlie finished his gin. The pair stood silent.

"Well," said Charlie, striking his leg. "Swelp me
bob! It fair beats me! Twins! Who'd ha' thought
it? Jos, lad, thou mays't be thankful as it isna' triplets.
Never did I think, as I was footing it up here this
morning, as it was twins I was coming to!"

"Hast got that half quid in thy pocket?"

"What half quid?" said Charlie defensively.

"Now then. Chuck us it over!" said Jos, suddenly
harsh and overbearing.

"I laid thee half quid as it 'ud be a wench," said
Charlie doggedly.

"Thou'rt a liar, Charlie!" said Jos. "Thou laid'st half a quid as it wasna' a boy."

"Nay, nay!" Charlie shook his head.

"And a boy it is!" Jos persisted.

"It being a lad *and* a wench," said Charlie, with a judicial air, "and me 'aving laid as it 'ud be a wench, I wins." In his accents and his gestures I could discern the mean soul, who on principle never paid until he was absolutely forced to pay. I could see also that Jos Myatt knew his man.

"Thou laidst me as it wasna' a lad," Jos almost shouted. "And a lad it is, I tell thee."

"*And* a wench!" said Charlie; then shook his head.

The wrangle proceeded monotonously, each party repeating over and over again the phrases of his own argument. I was very glad that Jos did not know me to be a witness of the making of the bet; otherwise I should assuredly have been summoned to give judgment.

"Let's call it off, then," Charlie suggested at length. "That'll settle it. And it being twins——"

"Nay, thou old devil, I'll none call it off. Thou owes me half a quid, and I'll have it out of thee."

"Look ye here," Charlie said more softly. "I'll tell thee what'll settle it. Which on 'em come first, th' lad or th' wench?"

"Th' wench come first," Jos Myatt admitted, with resentful reluctance, dully aware that defeat was awaiting him.

"Well, then! Th' wench is thy eldest child. That's law, that is. And what was us betting about, Jos lad? Us was betting about thy eldest and no other. I'll admit as I laid it wasna' a lad, as thou sayst. And it *wasna'* a lad. First come is eldest, and us was betting about eldest."

Charlie stared at the father in triumph.

Jos Myatt pushed roughly past him in the narrow space behind the bar, and came into the parlor. Nodding to me curtly, he unlocked the bookcase and took two crown pieces from a leathern purse which lay next to the bag. Then he returned to the bar, and banged the coins on the counter with fury.

"Take thy brass!" he shouted angrily. "Take thy brass! But thou'rt a damned shark, Charlie, and if anybody 'ud give me a plug o' bacca for doing it, I'd bash thy face in."

The other sniggered contentedly as he picked up his money.

"A bet's a bet," said Charlie.

He was clearly accustomed to an occasional violence of demeanor from Jos Myatt, and felt no fear. But he was wrong in feeling no fear. He had not allowed, in his estimate of the situation, for the exasperated condition of Jos Myatt's nerves under the unique experiences of the night.

Jos's face twisted into a hundred wrinkles and his hand seized Charlie by the arm whose hand held the coins.

"Drop 'em!" he cried loudly, repenting his naïve honesty. "Drop 'em! Or I'll——"

The stout woman, her apron all soiled, now came swiftly and scarce heard into the parlor, and stood at the door leading to the bar-room.

"What's up, Susannah?" Jos demanded in a new voice.

"Well may ye ask what's up!" said the woman. "Shouting and brangling there, ye sots!"

"What's up?" Jos demanded again, loosing Charlie's
arm.

"Her's gone!" the woman feebly whimpered, "Like
that!" with a vague movement of the hand indicating
suddenness. Then she burst into wild sobs, and rushed
madly back whence she had come, and the sound of
her sobs diminished as she ascended the stairs, and
expired altogether in the distant shutting of a door.

The men looked at each other.

Charlie restored the crown-pieces to the counter, and
pushed them towards Jos.

"Here!" he murmured faintly.

Jos flung them savagely to the ground. Another
pause followed.

"As God is my witness," he exclaimed solemnly, his
voice saturated with feeling, "As God is my witness,"
he repeated, "I'll ne'er touch a footba' again!"

Little Charlie gazed up at him sadly, plaintively, for
what seemed a long while.

"It's good-by to th' First League, then, for Knype!"
he tragically muttered, at length.

Chapter VIII

Dr. Stirling drove the car very slowly back to
Bursley. We glided gently down into the populous
valleys. All the stunted trees were coated with rime,
which made the sharpest contrast with their black
branches and the black mud under us. The high chimneys sent forth their black smoke calmly and tirelessly
into the fresh blue sky. Sunday had descended on the
vast landscape like a physical influence. We saw a
snake of children winding out of a dark brown Sunday
school into a dark brown chapel. And up from the

valleys came all the bells of all the temples of all the
different gods of the Five Towns, chiming, clanging,
ringing, each insisting that it alone invited to the altar
of the one God. And priests and acolytes of the various cults hurried occasionally along, in silk hats and
bright neckties, and smooth coats with folded handker-
chiefs sticking out of the pockets, busy, happy and
self-important, the convinced heralds of eternal salvation: no doubt nor hesitation as to any fundamental
truth had ever entered their minds. We passed through
a long, straight street of new red houses with blue slate
roofs, all gated and gardened. Here and there a girl
with her hair in pins and a rough brown apron over a
gaudy frock was stoning a front-step. And half-way
down the street a man in a scarlet jersey, supported by
two women in blue bonnets, was beating a drum and
crying aloud: "My friends, you may die to-night.
Where, I ask you, where——?" But he had no friends;
not even a boy heeded him. The drum continued to
bang in our rear.

I enjoyed all this. All this seemed to me to be fine,
seemed to throw off the true, fine, romantic savor of
life. I would have altered nothing in it. Mean, harsh,
ugly, squalid, crude, barbaric,—yes, but what an intoxi-
cating sense in it of the organized vitality of a vast
community unconscious of itself! I would have altered
nothing even in the events of the night. I thought of
the rooms at the top of the staircase of the Foaming
Quart,—mysterious rooms which I had not seen and
never should see, recondite rooms from which a soul
had slipped away and into which two had come, scenes
of anguish and of frustrated effort! Historical rooms,
surely! And yet not a house in the hundreds of houses
past which we slid but possessed rooms ennobled and

made august by happenings exactly as impressive in
their tremendous inexplicableness.

The natural humanity of Jos Myatt and Charlie,
their fashion of comporting themselves in a sudden
stress, pleased me. How else should they have be-
haved? I could understand Charlie's prophetic dirge
over the ruin of the Knype Football Club. It was not
that he did not feel the tragedy in the house. He had
felt it, and because he had felt it he had uttered at
random, foolishly, the first clear thought that ran into
his head.

Stirling was quiet. He appeared to be absorbed in
steering, and looked straight in front, yawning now and
again. He was much more fatigued than I was. Indeed
I had slept pretty well. He said as we swerved into
Trafalgar Road and overtook the aristocracy on its way
to chapel and church:

"Well, ye let yeself in for a night, young man! No
mistake!"

He smiled, and I smiled.

"What's going to occur up there?" I asked, indicating
Toft End.

"What do you mean?"

"A man like that—left with two babies!"

"Oh!" he said. "They'll manage that all right. His
sister's a widow. She'll go and live with him. She's as
fond of those infants already as if they were her own."

We drew up at his double gates.

"Be sure ye explain to Brindley," he said, as I left
him, "that it isn't my fault ye've had a night out of
bed. It was your own doing. I'm going to get a bit
of sleep now. See you this evening. Bob's asked me
to supper."

A servant was sweeping Bob Brindley's porch, and

the front door was open. I went in. The sound of the piano guided me to the drawing-room. Brindley, the morning cigaret between his lips, was playing one of Maurice Ravel's "Miroirs." He held his head back so as to keep the smoke out of his eyes. His children in their blue jerseys were building bricks on the carpet.

Without ceasing to play, he addressed me calmly:

"You're a nice chap! Where the devil have you been?"

And one of the little boys glancing up, said with roguish imitative innocence, in his high shrill voice:

"Where the del you been?"

THE SUBSTITUTE

By François Coppée

He was scarcely ten years old when he was first
arrested as a vagabond.

He spoke thus to the judge:

"I am called Jean François Leturc, and for six
months I was with the man who sings and plays upon
a cord of catgut between the lanterns at the Place de
la Bastille. I sang the refrain with him, and after
that I called, 'Here's all the new songs, ten centimes,
two sous!' He was always drunk, and used to beat
me. That is why the police picked me up the other
night. Before that I was with the man who sells
brushes. My mother was a laundress, her name was
Adèle. At one time she lived with a man on the
ground-floor at Montmartre. She was a good work-
woman and liked me. She made money because she
had for customers waiters in the cafés, and they use
a good deal of linen. On Sundays she used to put me
to bed early so that she could go to the ball. On
week-days she sent me to Les Frères, where I learned
to read. Well, the sergent-de-ville whose beat was in
our street used always to stop before our windows to
talk with her—a good-looking chap, with a medal
from the Crimea. They were married, and after that
everything went wrong. He didn't take to me, and
turned mother against me. Every one had a blow for

me, and so, to get out of the house, I spent whole days
in the Place Clichy, where I knew the mountebanks.
My father-in-law lost his place, and my mother her
work. She used to go out washing to take care of
him; this gave her a cough—the steam. . . . She is
dead at Lamboisière. She was a good woman. Since
that I have lived with the seller of brushes and the
catgut scraper. Are you going to send me to prison?"

He said this openly, cynically, like a man. He was
a little ragged street-arab, as tall as a boot, his forehead
hidden under a queer mop of yellow hair.

Nobody claimed him, and they sent him to the
Reform School.

Not very intelligent, idle, clumsy with his hands,
the only trade he could learn there was not a good
one—that of reseating straw chairs. However, he was
obedient, naturally quiet and silent, and he did not
seem to be profoundly corrupted by that school of
vice. But when, in his seventeenth year, he was thrown
out again on the streets of Paris, he unhappily found
there his prison comrades, all great scamps, exercising
their dirty professions: teaching dogs to catch rats
in the sewers, and blacking shoes on ball nights in the
passage of the Opera—amateur wrestlers, who permitted themselves to be thrown by the Hercules of
the booths—or fishing at noontime from rafts; all of
these occupations he followed to some extent, and,
some months after he came out of the house of cor-
rection, he was arrested again for a petty theft—a pair
of old shoes prigged from a shop-window. Result: a
year in the prison of Sainte Pélagie, where he served
as valet to the political prisoners.

He lived in much surprize among this group of
prisoners, all very young, negligent in dress, who talked

in loud voices, and carried their heads in a very solemn
fashion. They used to meet in the cell of one of the
oldest of them, a fellow of some thirty years, already
a long time in prison and quite a fixture at Sainte
Pélagie—a large cell, the walls covered with colored
caricatures, and from the window of which one could
see all Paris—its roofs, its spires, and its domes—and
far away the distant line of hills, blue and indistinct
upon the sky. There were upon the walls some shelves
filled with volumes and all the old paraphernalia of a
fencing-room: broken masks, rusty foils, breastplates,
and gloves that were losing their tow. It was there
that the "politicians" used to dine together, adding to
the everlasting "soup and beef," fruit, cheese, and
pints of wine which Jean François went out and got
by the can—a tumultous repast interrupted by violent
disputes, and where, during the dessert, the "Carmag-
nole" and "Ca Ira" were sung in full chorus. They
assumed, however, an air of great dignity on those
days when a newcomer was brought in among them,
at first entertaining him gravely as a citizen, but on
the morrow using him with affectionate familiarity
and calling him by his nickname. Great words were
used there: Corporation, Responsibility, and phrases
quite unintelligible to Jean François—such as this, for
example, which he once heard imperiously put forth
by a frightful little hunchback who blotted some writ-
ing-paper every night:

"It is done. This is the composition of the Cabinet:
Raymond, the Bureau of Public Instruction; Martial,
the Interior; and for Foreign Affairs, myself."

His time done, he wandered again around Paris,
watched afar by the police, after the fashion of cock-
chafers, made by cruel children to fly at the end of a

string. He became one of those fugitive and timid
beings whom the law, with a sort of coquetry, arrests
and releases by turn—something like those platonic
fishers who, in order that they may not exhaust their
fish-pond, throw immediately back into the water the
fish which has just come out of the net. Without a
suspicion on his part that so much honor had been
done to so sorry a subject, he had a special bundle of
memoranda in the mysterious portfolios of the Rue
de Jérusalem. His name was written in round hand
on the gray paper of the cover, and the notes and
reports, carefully classified, gave him his successive
appellations: "Name, Leturc"; "the prisoner Leturc,"
and, at last, "the criminal Leturc."

He was two years out of prison, dining where he
could, sleeping in night lodging-houses and sometimes
in lime-kilns, and taking part with his fellows in
interminable games of pitch-penny on the boulevards
near the barriers. He wore a greasy cap on the back
of his head, carpet slippers, and a short white blouse.
When he had five sous he had his hair curled. He
danced at Constant's at Montparnasse; bought for
two sous to sell for four at the door of Bobino, the
jack of hearts or the ace of clubs serving as a counter-
mark; sometimes opened the door of a carriage; led
horses to the horse-market. From the lottery of all
sorts of miserable employments he drew a goodly
number. Who can say if the atmosphere of honor
which one breathes as a soldier, if military discipline
might not have saved him? Taken, in a cast of the
net, with some young loafers who robbed drunkards
sleeping on the streets, he denied very earnestly having taken part in their expeditions. Perhaps he told
the truth, but his antecedents were accepted in lieu

of proof, and he was sent for three years to Poissy. There he made coarse playthings for children, was tattooed on the chest, learned thieves' slang and the penal code. A new liberation, and a new plunge into the sink of Paris; but very short this time, for at the end of six months at the most he was again compromised in a night robbery, aggravated by climbing and breaking —a serious affair, in which he played an obscure rôle, half dupe and half fence. On the whole his complicity was evident, and he was sent for five years at hard labor. His grief in this adventure was above all in being separated from an old dog which he had found on a dung-heap and cured of the mange. The beast loved him.

Toulon, the ball and chain, the work in the harbor, the blows from a stick, wooden shoes on bare feet, soup of black beans dating from Trafalgar, no tobacco money, and the terrible sleep in a camp swarming with convicts; that was what he experienced for five broiling summers and five winters raw with the Mediterranean wind. He came out from there stunned, was sent under surveillance to Vernon, where he worked some time on the river. Then, an incorrigible vagabond, he broke his exile and came again to Paris. He had his savings, fifty-six francs, that is to say, time enough for reflection. During his absence his former wretched companions had dispersed. He was well hidden, and slept in a loft at an old woman's, to whom he represented himself as a sailor, tired of the sea, who had lost his papers in a recent shipwreck, and who wanted to try his hand at something else. His tanned face and his calloused hands, together with some sea phrases which he dropped from time to time, made his tale seem probable enough.

One day when he risked a saunter in the streets, and when chance had led him as far as Montmartre, where he was born, an unexpected memory stopped him before the door of Les Frères, where he had learned to read. As it was very warm the door was open, and by a single glance the passing outcast was able to recognize the peaceable school-room. Nothing was changed: neither the bright light shining in at the great windows, nor the crucifix over the desk, nor the rows of benches with the tables furnished with ink-stands and pencils, nor the table of weights and measures, nor the map where pins stuck in still indicated the operations of some ancient war. Heedlessly and without thinking, Jean François read on the blackboard the words of the Evangelist which had been set there as a copy:

"Joy shall be in heaven over one sinner that repenteth, more than over ninety and nine just persons, which need no repentance."

It was undoubtedly the hour for recreation, for the Brother Professor had left his chair, and, sitting on the edge of a table, he was telling a story to the boys who surrounded him with eager and attentive eyes. What a bright and innocent face he had, that beardless young man, in his long black gown, and white necktie, and great ugly shoes, and his badly cut brown hair streaming out behind! All the simple figures of the children of the people who were watching him seemed scarcely less childlike than his; above all when, delighted with some of his own simple and priestly pleasantries, he broke out in an open and frank peal of laughter which showed his white and regular teeth, a peal so contagious that all the scholars laughed loudly in their turn. It was such a sweet, simple group in the bright sunlight, which lighted their dear eyes and their blond curls.

Jean François looked at them for some time in silence, and for the first time in that savage nature, all instinct and appetite, there awoke a mysterious, a tender emotion. His heart, that seared and hardened heart, unmoved when the convict's cudgel or the heavy whip of the watchman fell on his shoulders, beat oppressively. In that sight he saw again his infancy; and closing his eyes sadly, the prey to torturing regret, he walked quickly away.

Then the words written on the blackboard came back to his mind.

"If it wasn't too late, after all!" he murmured; "if I could again, like others, eat honestly my brown bread, and sleep my fill without nightmare! The spy must be sharp who recognizes me. My beard, which I shaved off down there, has grown out thick and strong. One can burrow somewhere in the great ant-hill, and work can be found. Whoever is not worked to death in the hell of the galleys comes out agile and robust, and I learned there to climb ropes with loads upon my back. Building is going on everywhere here, and the masons need helpers. Three francs a day! I never earned so much. Let me be forgotten, and that is all I ask."

He followed his courageous resolution; he was faithful to it, and after three months he was another man. The master for whom he worked called him his best workman. After a long day upon the scaffolding, in the hot sun and the dust, constantly bending and raising his back to take the hod from the man at his feet and pass it to the man over his head, he went for his soup to the cook-shop, tired out, his legs aching.

his hands burning, his eyelids stuck with plaster, but
content with himself, and carrying his well-earned
money in a knot in his handkerchief. He went out
now without fear, since he could not be recognized
in white mask, and since he had noticed that the
suspicious glances of the policeman were seldom turned
on the tired workman. He was quiet and sober. He
slept the sound sleep of fatigue. He was free!

At last—oh, supreme recompense!—he had a friend!

He was a fellow-workman like himself, named Savinien, a little peasant with red lips who had come to
Paris with his stick over his shoulder and a bundle on
the end of it, fleeing from the wine-shops and going
to mass every Sunday. Jean François loved him for
his piety, for his candor, for his honesty, for all that
he himself had lost, and so long ago. It was a passion,
profound and unrestrained, which transformed him by
fatherly cares and attentions. Savinien, himself of a
weak and egotistical nature, let things take their course
satisfied only in finding a companion who shared his
horror of the wine-shop. The two friends lived together in a fairly comfortable lodging, but their re-
sources were very limited. They were obliged to take
into their room a third companion, an old Auvergnat,
gloomy and rapacious, who found it possible out of his
meager salary to save something with which to buy a
place in his own country. Jean François and Savinien
were always together. On holidays they together
took long walks in the environs of Paris, and dined
under an arbor in one of those small country inns
where there are great many mushrooms in the sauces
and innocent rebusses on the napkins. There Jean
François learned from his friend all that lore of which
they who are born in the city are ignorant; learned

the names of the trees, the flowers, and the plants;
the various seasons for harvestings; he heard eagerly
the thousand details of a laborious country life—the
autumn sowing, the winter chores, the splendid celebra-
tions of harvest and vintage days, the sound of the
mills at the water-side, and the flails striking the
ground, the tired horses led to water, and the hunting
in the morning mist; and, above all, the long even-
ings around the fire of vine-shoots, that were shortened
by some marvelous stories. He discovered in himself
a source of imagination before unknown, and found a
singular delight in the recital of events so placid, so
calm, so monotonous.

One thing troubled him, however; it was the fear
lest Savinien might learn something of his past. Sometimes there escaped from him some low word of
thieves' slang, a vulgar gesture—vestiges of his former
horrible existence—and he felt the pain one feels when
old wounds reopen; the more because he fancied that
he sometimes saw in Savinien the awakening of an
unhealthy curiosity. When the young man, already
tempted by the pleasures which Paris offers to the
poorest, asked him about the mysteries of the great
city, Jean François feigned ignorance and turned
the subject; but he felt a vague inquietude for the
future of his friend.

His uneasiness was not without foundation. Savinien could not long remain the simple rustic that he
was on his arrival in Paris. If the gross and noisy
pleasures of the wine-shop always repelled him, he
was profoundly troubled by other temptations, full of
danger for the inexperience of his twenty years. When
spring came he began to go off alone, and at first he
wandered about the brilliant entrance of some danc·

ing-hall, watching the young girls who went in with
their arms around each other's waists, talking in low
tones. Then, one evening, when lilacs perfumed the
air and the call to quadrilles was most captivating,
he crossed the threshold, and from that time Jean
François observed a change, little by little, in his
manners and his visage. He became more frivolous,
more extravagant. He often borrowed from his friend
his scanty savings, and he forgot to repay. Jean
François, feeling that he was abandoned, jealous and
forgiving at the same time, suffered and was silent.
He felt that he had no right to reproach him, but
with the foresight of affection he indulged in cruel
and inevitable presentiments.

One evening, as he was mounting the stairs to his
room, absorbed in his thoughts, he heard, as he was
about to enter, the sound of angry voices, and he
recognized that of the old Auvergnat who lodged with
Savinien and himself. An old habit of suspicion made
him stop at the landing-place and listen to learn the
cause of the trouble.

"Yes," said the Auvergnat, angrily, "I am sure that
some one has opened my trunk and stolen from it the
three louis that I had hidden in a little box; and he
who has done this thing must be one of the two
companions who sleep here, if it were not the servant
Maria. It concerns you as much as it does me, since
you are the master of the house, and I will drag you
to the courts if you do not let me at once break open
the valises of the two masons. My poor gold! It
was here yesterday in its place, and I will tell you
just what it was, so that if we find it again nobody
can accuse me of having lied. Ah, I know them, my
three beautiful gold-pieces, and I can see them as

plainly as I see you! One piece was more worn than
the others; it was of greenish gold, with a portrait of
the great emperor. The other was a great old fellow
with a queue and epaulets; and the third, which had
on it a Philippe with whiskers, I had marked with
my teeth. They don't trick me. Do you know that
I only wanted two more like that to pay for my vine-
yard? Come, search these fellows' things with me,
or I will call the police! Hurry up!"

"All right," said the voice of the landlord; "we
will go and search with Maria. So much the worse
for you if we find nothing, and the masons get angry.
You have forced me to it."

Jean François' soul was full of fright. He remembered the embarrassed circumstances and the small
loans of Savinien and how sober he had seemed for
some days. And yet he could not believe that he was
a thief. He heard the Auvergnat panting in his eager
search, and he pressed his closed fists against his
breast as if to still the furious beating of his heart.

"Here they are!" suddenly shouted the victorious
miser. "Here they are, my louis, my dear treasure;
and in the Sunday vest of that little hypocrite of
Limousin! Look, landlord, they are just as I told
you. Here is the Napoleon, the man with a queue,
and the Philippe that I have bitten. See the dents!
Ah, the little beggar with the sanctified air. I should
have much sooner suspected the other. Ah, the wretch!
Well, he must go to the convict prison."

At this moment Jean François heard the well-known
step of Savinien coming slowly up the stairs.

He is going to his destruction, thought he. Three
stories. I have time!

And, pushing open the door, he entered the room,

pale as death, where he saw the landlord and the servant stupefied in a corner, while the Auvergnat, on his knees, in the disordered heap of clothes, was kissing the pieces of gold.

"Enough of this," he said, in a thick voice; "I took the money, and put it in my comrade's trunk. But that is too bad. I am a thief, but not a Judas. Call the police; I will not try to escape, only I must say a word to Savinien in private. Here he is."

In fact, the little Limousin had just arrived, and seeing his crime discovered, believing himself lost, he stood there, his eyes fixed, his arms hanging.

Jean François seized him forcibly by the neck, as if to embrace him; he put his mouth close to Savinien's ear, and said to him in a low, supplicating voice:

"Keep quiet."

Then turning towards the others:

"L ave me alone with him. I tell you I won't go away. Lock us in if you wish, but leave us alone."

With a commanding gesture he showed them the door.

They went out.

Savinien, broken by grief, was sitting on the bed, and lowered his eyes without understanding anything.

"Listen," said Jean François, who came and took him by the hands. "I understand! You have stolen three gold-pieces to buy some trifle for a girl. That costs six months in prison. But one only comes out from there to go back again, and you will become a pillar of police courts and tribunals. I understand it. I have been seven years at the Reform School, a year at Sainte Pélagie, three years at Poissy, five years at Toulon. Now, don't be afraid. Everything is arranged. I have taken it on my shoulders."

"It is dreadful," said Savinien; but hope was springing up again in his cowardly heart.

"When the elder brother is under the flag, the younger one does not go," replied Jean François. "I am your substitute, that's all. You care for me a little, do you not? I am paid. Don't be childish—don't refuse. They would have taken me again one of these days, for I am a runaway from exile. And then, do you see, that life will be less hard for me than for you. I know it all, and I shall not complain if I have not done you this service for nothing, and if you swear to me that you will never do it again. Savinien, I have loved you well, and your friendship has made me happy. It is through it that, since I have known you, I have been honest and pure, as I might always have been, perhaps, if I had had, like you, a father to put a tool in my hands, a mother to teach me my prayers. It was my sole regret that I was useless to you, and that I deceived you concerning myself. To-day I have unmasked in saving you. It is all right. Do not cry, and embrace me, for already I hear heavy boots on the stairs. They are coming with the *posse*, and we must not seem to know each other so well before those chaps."

He pressed Savinien quickly to his breast, then pushed him from him, when the door was thrown wide open.

It was the landlord and the Auvergnat, who brought the police. Jean François sprang forward to the landing-place, held out his hands for the handcuffs, and said, laughing, "Forward, bad lot!"

To-day he is at Cayenne, condemned for life as an incorrigible.

THE CLOAK

By Nikolai Vasilievitch Gogol

In the department of—but it is better not to men-
tion the department. There is nothing more irritable
than departments, regiments, courts of justice, and, in
a word, every branch of public service. Each individual attached to them nowadays thinks all society
insulted in his person. Quite recently a complaint
was received from a justice of the peace, in which he
plainly demonstrated that all the imperial institutions
were going to the dogs, and that the Czar's sacred
name was being taken in vain; and in proof he ap-
pended to the complaint a romance, in which the
justice of the peace is made to appear about once in
every ten lines, and sometimes in a drunken condition. Therefore, in order to avoid all unpleasantness,
it will be better to designate the department in question as a certain department.

So, in a certain department there was a certain
official—not a very high one, it must be allowed—
short of stature, somewhat pock-marked, red-haired,
and short-sighted, with a bald forehead, wrinkled
cheeks, and a complexion of the kind known as
sanguine. The St. Petersburg climate was responsible
for this. As for his official status, he was what is
called a perpetual titular councilor, over which some
writers make merry and crack their jokes, obeying

the praiseworthy custom of attacking those who can not bite back.

His family name was Bashmatchkin. This name is evidently derived from *bashmak* (shoe); but when, at what time, and in what manner, is not known. His father and grandfather, and all the Bashmatchkins, always wore boots, which only had new heels two or three times a year. His name was Akakiy Akakievitch. It may strike the reader as rather singular and far-fetched! but he may rest assured that it was by no means far-fetched, and that the circumstances were such that it would have been impossible to give him any other.

This was how it came about.

Akakiy Akakievitch was born, if my memory fails me not, in the evening on the 23d of March. His mother, the wife of a Government official, and a very fine woman, made all due arrangements for having the child baptized. She was lying on the bed opposite the door; on her right stood the godfather, Ivan Ivanovitch Eroshkin, a most estimable man, who served as presiding officer of the senate; and the godmother, Anna Semenovna Byelobrushkova, the wife of an officer of the quarter, and a woman of rare virtues. They offered the mother her choice of three names, Mokiya, Sossiya, or that the child should be called after the martyr Khozdazat. "No," said the good woman, "all those names are poor." In order to please her, they opened the calendar at another place; three more names appeared, Triphiliy, Dula, and Varakhasiy. "This is a judgment," said the old woman. "What names! I truly never heard the like. Varadat or Varukh might have been borne, but not Triphiliy and Varakhasiy!" They turned to another

page and found Pavsikakhiy and Vakhtisiy. "Now
I see," said the old woman, "that it is plainly fate.
And since such is the case, it will be better to name
him after his father. His father's name was Akakiy,
so let his son's be Akakiy too." In this manner he
became Akakiy Akakievitch. They christened the
child, whereat he wept, and made a grimace, as tho
he foresaw that he was to be a titular councilor.

In this manner did it all come about. We have
mentioned it in order that the reader might see for
himself that it was a case of necessity, and that it was
utterly impossible to give him any other name. When
and how he entered the department, and who appointed
him, no one could remember. However much the
directors and chiefs of all kinds were changed, he was
always to be seen in the same place, the same attitude,
the same occupation; so that it was afterward affirmed
that he had been born in undress uniform with a bald
head.

No respect was shown him in the department. The
porter not only did not rise from his seat when he
passed, but never even glanced at him, any more than
if a fly had flown through the reception-room. His
superiors treated him in coolly despotic fashion. Some
subchief would thrust a paper under his nose without
so much as saying "Copy," or "Here's a nice, interesting affair," or anything else agreeable, as is cus-
tomary among well-bred officials. And he took it,
looking only at the paper, and not observing who
handed it to him, or whether he had the right to do
so; simply took it, and set about copying it.

The young officials laughed at and made fun of him,
so far as their official wit permitted; told in his presence various stories concocted about him, and about

his landlady, an old woman of seventy; declared that
she beat him; asked when the wedding was to be;
and strewed bits of paper over his head, calling them
snow. But Akakiy Akakievitch answered not a word,
any more than if there had been no one there besides
himself. It even had no effect upon his work: amid
all these annoyances he never made a single mistake
in a letter. But if the joking became wholly unbearable, as when they jogged his hand, and prevented his attending to his work, he would exclaim,
"Leave me alone! Why do you insult me?" And
there was something strange in the words and the voice
in which they were uttered. There was in it something which moved to pity; so much that one young
man, a newcomer, who, taking pattern by the others,
had permitted himself to make sport of Akakiy, suddenly stopped short, as tho all about him had under-
gone a transformation and presented itself in a different aspect. Some unseen force repelled him from the
comrades whose acquaintance he had made, on the
supposition that they were well-bred and polite men.
Long afterward, in his gayest moments, there recurred
to his mind the little official with the bald forehead,
with his heart-rending words, "Leave me alone! Why
do you insult me?" In these moving words, other
words resounded—"I am thy brother." And the young
man covered his face with his hand; and many a time
afterward, in the course of his life, shuddered at seeing
how much inhumanity there is in man, how much
savage coarseness is concealed beneath delicate, re-
fined worldliness, and even, O God! in that man whom
the world acknowledges as honorable and noble.

It would be difficult to find another man who lived
so entirely for his duties. It is not enough to say

that Akakiy labored with zeal: no, he labored with
love. In his copying he found a varied and agreeable
employment. Enjoyment was written on his face:
some letters were even favorites with him, and when
he encountered these he smiled, winked, and worked
with his lips, till it seemed as tho each letter might
be read in his face, as his pen traced it. If his pay
had been in proportion to his zeal, he would, perhaps,
to his great surprise, have been made even a councilor
of state, But he worked, as his companions, the wits,
put it, like a horse in a mill.

Moreover, it is impossible to say that no attention
was paid to him. One director, being a kindly man,
and desirous of rewarding him for his long service,
ordered him to be given something more important
than mere copying. So he was ordered to make a
report of an already concluded affair to another department; the duty consisting simply in changing the
heading and altering a few words from the first to the
third person. This caused him so much toil that he
broke into a perspiration, rubbed his forehead, and
finally said: "No, give me rather something to copy."
After that they let him copy on forever.

Outside this copying, it appeared that nothing existed
for him. He gave no thought to his clothes; his
undress uniform was not green, but a sort of rusty-
meal color. The collar was low, so that his neck, in
spite of the fact that it was not long, seemed in-
ordinately so as it emerged from it, like the necks of
those plaster cats which wag their heads and are
carried about upon the heads of scores of image
sellers. And something was always sticking to his
uniform, either a bit of hay or some trifle. Moreover, he had a peculiar knack, as he walked along the

street, of arriving beneath a window just as all sorts
of rubbish was being flung out of it; hence he always
bore about on his hat scraps of melon rinds and other
such articles.   Never once in his life did he give heed
to what was going on every day in the street; while
it is well known that his young brother officials train
the range of their glances till they can see when any
one's trouser-straps come undone upon the opposite
sidewalk, which always brings a malicious smile to
their faces.   But Akakiy Akakievitch saw in all things
the clean, even strokes of his written lines; and only
when a horse thrust his nose, from some unknown
quarter, over his shoulder, and sent a whole gust of
wind down his neck from his nostrils, did he observe
that he was not in the middle of a page, but in the
middle of the street.

On reaching home he sat down at once at the table,
supped his cabbage-soup up quickly, and swallowed a
bit of beef with onions, never noticing their taste, and
gulping down everything with flies and anything else
which the Lord happened to send at the moment.   His
stomach filled, he rose from the table and copied
papers which he had brought home.   If there happened
to be none, he took copies for himself, for his own
gratification, especially if the document was noteworthy, not on account of its style, but of its being
addressed to some distinguished person.

Even at the hour when the gray St. Petersburg sky
had quite disappeared, and all the official world had
eaten or dined, each as he could, in accordance with
the salary he received and his own fancy; when all
were resting from the department jar of pens, running to and fro from their own and other people's
indispensable occupations, and from all the work that

an uneasy man makes willingly for himself, rather
than what is necessary; when officials hasten to dedicate
to pleasure the time which is left to them, one bolder
than the rest going to the theater; another into the
street, looking under all the bonnets; another wasting
his evening in compliments to some pretty girl, the
star of a small official circle: another—and this is the
common case of all—visiting his comrades on the fourth
or third floor, in two small rooms with an anteroom
or kitchen, and some pretensions to fashion, such as
a lamp or some other trifle, which has cost many a
sacrifice of dinner or pleasure trip; in a word, at the
hour when all officials disperse among the contracted
quarters of their friends, to play whist as they sip
their tea from glasses with a kopek's worth of sugar,
smoke long pipes, relate at times some bits of gossip
which a Russian man can never, under any circumstances, refrain from, and, when there is nothing else
to talk of, repeat eternal anecdotes about the com-
mandant to whom they had sent word that the tails
of the horses on the Falconet Monument had been
cut off, when all strive to divert themselves, Akakiy
Akakievitch indulged in no kind of diversion. No one
could ever say that he had seen him at any kind of
evening party. Having written to his heart's content,
he lay down to sleep, smiling at the thought of the
coming day—of what God might send him to copy
on the morrow.

Thus flowed on the peaceful life of the man, who,
with a salary of four hundred rubles, understood how
to be content with his lot; and thus it would have
continued to flow on, perhaps, to extreme old age
were it not that there are various ills strewn along
the path of life for titular councilors as well as for

private, actual, court, and every other species of councilor, even for those who never give any advice or take any themselves.

There exists in St. Petersburg a powerful foe of all who receive a salary of four hundred rubles a year, or thereabouts. This foe is no other than the northern cold, altho it is said to be very healthy. At nine o'clock in the morning, at the very hour when the streets are filled with men bound for the various official departments, it begins to bestow such powerful and piercing nips on all noses impartially that the poor officials really do not know what to do with them. At an hour when the foreheads of even those who occupy exalted positions ache with the cold, and tears start to their eyes, the poor titular councilors are sometimes quite unprotected. Their only salvation lies in traversing as quickly as possible, in their thin little cloaks, five or six streets, and then warming their feet in the porter's room, and so thawing all their talents and qualifications for official service which had become frozen on the way.

Akakiy Akakievitch had felt for some time that his back and shoulders suffered with peculiar poignancy in spite of the fact that he tried to traverse the distance with all possible speed. He began finally to wonder whether the fault did not lie in his cloak. He examined it thoroughly at home, and discovered that in two places, namely, on the back and shoulders, it had become thin as gauze; the cloth was worn to such a degree that he could see through it, and the lining had fallen into pieces. You must know that Akakiy Akakievitch's cloak served as an object of ridicule to the officials; they even refused it the noble name of cloak, and called it a cane. In fact, it was of singular make; its collar diminishing year by year, but serving to patch its other parts. The patching did not exhibit great skill on the part of the tailor, and was, in fact, baggy and ugly. Seeing how the matter stood, Akakiy Akakievitch decided that it would be necessary to take the cloak to Petrovitch, the tailor, who lived somewhere on the fourth floor, up a dark staircase, and who, in spite of his having but one eye, and pock-marks all over his face, busied himself in repairing the trousers and coats of officials and others; that is to say, when he was sober, and not nursing some other scheme in his head.

It is not necessary to say much about this tailor; but, as it is the custom to have the character of each personage in a novel clearly defined, there is no help for it, so here is Petrovitch the tailor. At first he was called only Grigoriv, and was some gentleman's serf; he commenced calling himself Petrovitch from the time when he received his free papers, and further began to drink heavily on all holidays, at first on the great ones, and then on all church festivals without discrimination, wherever a cross stood in the calendar. On this point he was faithful to ancestral custom; and when quarreling with his wife he called her a low female and a German. As we have mentioned his wife, it will be necessary to say a word or two about her. Unfortunately, little is known of her beyond the fact that Petrovitch has a wife, who wears a cap and a dress, but can not lay claim to beauty; at least, no one but the soldiers of the guard even looked under her cap when they met her.

Ascending the staircase which led to Petrovitch's room—which staircase was all soaked with dish-water and reeked with the smell of spirits which affects the

eyes, and is an inevitable adjunct to all dark stair-
ways in St. Petersburg houses—ascending the stairs,
Akakiy Akakievitch pondered how much Petrovitch
would ask, and mentally resolved not to give more
than two rubles. The door was open; for the mistress, in cooking some fish, had raised such a smoke
in the kitchen that not even the beetles were visible.
Akakiy Akakievitch passed through the kitchen un-
perceived, even by the housewife, and at length reached
a room where he beheld Petrovitch seated on a large
unpainted table, with his legs tucked under him like
a Turkish pasha. His feet were bare, after the fashion
of tailors as they sit at work; and the first thing
which caught the eye was his thumb, with a deformed
nail thick and strong as a turtle's shell. About
Petrovitch's neck hung a skein of silk and thread,
and upon his knees lay some old garment. He had
been trying unsuccessfully for three minutes to thread
his needle, and was enraged at the darkness and even
at the thread, growling in a low voice, "It won't go
through, the barbarian! You pricked me, you rascal!"

Akakiy Akaievitch was vexed at arriving at the
precise moment when Petrovitch was angry; he liked
to order something of Petrovitch when the latter was
a little downhearted, or, as his wife expressed it,
"when he had settled himself with brandy, the one-
eyed devil!" Under such circumstances, Petrovitch
generally came down in his price very readily, and even
bowed and returned thanks. Afterward, to be sure,
his wife would come, complaining that her husband
was drunk, and so had fixed the price too low; but
if only a ten-kopek piece were added, then the matter
was settled. But now it appeared that Petrovitch
was in a sober condition, and therefore rough, taciturn,

and inclined to demand, Satan only knows what price.
Akakiy Akakievitch felt this, and would gladly have
beat a retreat; but he was in for it. Petrovitch
screwed up his one eye very intently at him; and
Akakiy Akakievitch involuntarily said: "How do you
do, Petrovitch?"

"I wish you a good-morning, sir," said Petrovitch,
squinting at Akakiy Akakievitch's hands, to see what
sort of booty he had brought.

"Ah! I—to you, Petrovitch, this—" It must be
known that Akakiy Akakievitch expressed himself
chiefly by prepositions, adverbs, and scraps of phrases
which had no meaning whatever. If the matter was
a very difficult one, he had a habit of never com-
pleting his sentences; so that frequently, having begun
a phrase with the words, "This, in fact, is quite—"
he forgot to go on, thinking that he had already finished
it.

"What is it?" asked Petrovitch, and with his one
eye scanned Akakievitch's whole uniform from the
collar down to the cuffs, the back, the tails, and the
button-holes, all of which were well known to him,
since they were his own handiwork. Such is the
habit of tailors; it is the first thing they do on meeting one.

"But I, here, this—Petrovitch—a cloak, cloth—here
you see, everywhere, in different places, it is quite
strong—it is a little dusty, and looks old, but it is
new, only here in one place it is a little—on the back,
and here on one of the shoulders, it is a little worn,
yes, here on this shoulder it is a little—do you see?
that is all. And a little work—"

Petrovitch took the cloak, spread it out, to begin
with, on the table, looked hard at it, shook his head,

reached out his hand to the window-sill for his snuff-box, adorned with the portrait of some general, tho what general is unknown, for the place where the face should have been had been rubbed through by the finger, and a square bit of paper had been pasted over it. Having taken a pinch of snuff, Petrovitch held up the cloak, and inspected it against the light, and again shook his head. Then he turned it, lining upward, and shook his head once more. After which he again lifted the general-adorned lid with its bit of pasted paper, and, having stuffed his nose with snuff, closed and put away the snuff-box, and said finally, "No, it is impossible to mend it; it's a wretched garment!"

Akakiy Akakievitch's heart sank at these words.

"Why is it impossible, Petrovitch?" he said, almost in the pleading voice of a child; "all that ails it is that it is worn at the shoulders. You must have some pieces—"

"Yes, patches could be found, patches are easily found," said Petrovitch, "but there's nothing to sew them to. The thing is completely rotten; if you put a needle to it—see, it will give way."

"Let it give way, and you can put on another patch at once."

"But there is nothing to put the patches on to; there's no use in strengthening it; it is too far gone. It's lucky that it's cloth; for, if the wind were to blow, it would fly away."

"Well, strengthen it again. How this, in fact."

"No," said Petrovitch decisively, "there is nothing to be done with it. It's a thoroughly bad job. You'd better, when the cold winter comes on, make yourself some gaiters out of it, because stockings are not warm.

The Germans invented them in order to make more money." Petrovitch loved, on all occasions, to have a fling at the Germans. "But it is plain you must have a new cloak."

At the word "new," all grew dark before Akakiy Akakievitch's eyes and everything in the room began to whirl round. The only thing he saw clearly was the general with the paper face on the lid of Petrovitch's snuff-box. "A new one?" said he, as if still in a dream; "why, I have no money for that."

"Yes, a new one," said Petrovitch, with barbarous composure.

"Well, if came to a new one, how it?"

"You mean how much would it cost?"

"Yes."

"Well, you would have to lay out a hundred and fifty or more," said Petrovitch, and pursed up his lips significantly. He liked to produce powerful effects, liked to stun utterly and suddenly and then to glance sidewise to see what face the stunned person would put on the matter.

"A hundred and fifty rubles for a cloak!" shrieked poor Akakiy Akakievitch, perhaps for the first time in his life, for his voice had always been distinguished for softness.

"Yes, sir," said Petrovitch, "for any kind of cloak. If you have a marten fur on the collar, or a silk-lined hood, it will mount up to two hundred."

"Petrovitch, please," said Akakiy Akakievitch in a beseeching tone, not hearing, and not trying to hear, Petrovitch's words, and disregarding all his "effects," "some repairs, in order that it may wear yet a little longer."

"No, it would only be a waste of time and money,"

said Petrovitch; and Akakiy Akakievitch went away
after these words, utterly discouraged. But Petrovitch stood for some time after his departure, with
significantly compressed lips, and without betaking
himself to his work, satisfied that he would not be
dropped, and an artistic tailor employed.

Akakiy Akakievitch went out into the street as if
in a dream. "Such an affair!" he said to himself: "I
did not think it had come to—" and then after a pause
he added: "Well, so it is! see what it has come to at
last! and I never imagined that it was so!" Then
followed a long silence, after which he exclaimed:
"Well, so it is! see what already—nothing unexpected
that it would be nothing—what a strange circumstance!" So saying, instead of going home, he went
in exactly the opposite direction without himself sus-
pecting it. On the way a chimney-sweep bumped up
against him and blackened his shoulder, and a whole
hatful of rubbish landed on him from the top of a
house which was building. He did not notice it; and
only when he ran against a watchman, who, having
planted his halberd beside him, was shaking some snuff
from his box into his horny hand, did he recover
himself a little, and that because the watchman said,
"Why are you poking yourself into a man's very face?
Haven't you the pavement?" This caused him to look
about him, and turn toward home.

There only he finally began to collect his thoughts
and to survey his position in its clear and actual light,
and to argue with himself, sensibly and frankly, as
with a reasonable friend, with whom one can discuss
private and personal matters. "No," said Akakiy
Akakievitch, "it is impossible to reason with Petrovitch now; he is that—evidently his wife has been

beating him. I'd better go to him on Sunday morning; after Saturday night he will be a little cross-eyed and sleepy, for he will want to get drunk, and his wife won't give him any money; and at such a time a ten-kopek piece in his hand will—he will become more fit to reason with, and then the cloak, and that—" Thus argued Akakiy Akakievitch with himself, regained his courage, and waited until the first Sunday, when, seeing from afar that Petrovitch's wife had left the house, he went straight to him.

Petrovitch's eye was, indeed, very much askew after Saturday: his head drooped and he was very sleepy; but for all that, as soon as he knew what it was a question of, it seemed as though Satan jogged his memory. "Impossible," said he; "please to order a new one." Thereupon Akakiy Akakievitch handed over the ten-kopek piece. "Thank you, sir; I will drink your good health," said Petrovitch; "but as for the cloak, don't trouble yourself about it; it is good for nothing. I will make you a capital new one, so let us settle about it now."

Akakiy Akakievitch was still for mending it; but Petrovitch would not hear of it, and said: "I shall certainly have to make you a new one, and you may depend upon it that I shall do my best. It may even be, as the fashion goes, that the collar can be fastened by silver hooks under a flap."

Then Akakiy Akakievitch saw that it was impossible to get along without a new cloak, and his spirit sank utterly. How, in fact, was it to be done? Where was the money to come from? He might, to be sure, depend, in part, upon his present at Christmas; but that money had long been allotted beforehand. He must have some new trousers, and pay a debt of long

standing to the shoemaker for putting new tops to his
old boots, and he must order three shirts from the
seamstress, and a couple of pieces of linen. In short,
all his money must be spent; and even if the director
should be so kind as to order him to receive forty-five
rubles instead of forty, or even fifty, it would be a
mere nothing, a mere drop in the ocean toward the
funds necessary for a cloak; altho he knew that
Petrovitch was often wrong-headed enough to blurt
out some outrageous price, so that even his own wife
could not refrain from exclaiming, "Have you lost your
senses, you fool?" At one time he would not work
at any price, and now it was quite likely that he had
named a higher sum than the cloak would cost.

But altho he knew that Petrovitch would under-
take to make a cloak for eighty rubles, still, where was
he to get the eighty rubles from? He might possibly
manage half; yes, half might be procured, but where
was the other half to come from? But the reader
must first be told where the first half came from.
Akakiy Akakievitch had a habit of putting, for every
ruble he spent, a kopek into a small box, fastened
with lock and key, and with a slit in the top for the
reception of money. At the end of every half-year he
counted over the heap of coppers, and changed it for
silver. This he had done for a long time, and in the
course of years the sum had mounted up to over forty
rubles. Thus he had one-half on hand; but where was
he to find the other half? where was he to get another
forty rubles from? Akakiy Akakievitch thought and
thought, and decided that it would be necessary to cur-
tail his ordinary expenses for the space of one year
at least—to dispense with tea in the evening, to burn
no candles, and, if there was anything which he must

do, to go into his landlady's room and work by her
light. When he went into the street he must walk as
lightly as he could, and as cautiously, upon the stones,
almost upon tiptoe, in order not to wear his heels down
in too short a time; he must give the laundress as little
to wash as possible; and, in order not to wear out his
clothes, he must take them off as soon as he got home,
and wear only his cotton dressing-gown, which had
been long and carefully saved.

To tell the truth, it was a little hard for him at first
to accustom himself to these deprivations; but he got
used to them at length, after a fashion, and all went
smoothly. He even got used to being hungry in the
evening, but he made up for it by treating himself,
so to say, in spirit, by bearing ever in mind the idea
of his future cloak. From that time forth his existence
seemed to become, in some way, fuller, as if he were
married, or as if some other man lived in him, as if,
in fact, he were not alone, and some pleasant friend
had consented to travel along life's path with him, the
friend being no other than the cloak, with thick wad-
ding and a strong lining incapable of wearing out. He
became more lively, and even his character grew
firmer, like that of a man who has made up his mind
and set himself a goal. From his face and gait, doubt
and indecision, all hesitating and wavering traits, disappeared of themselves. Fire gleamed in his eyes, and
occasionally the boldest and most daring ideas flitted
through his mind; why not, for instance, have marten
fur on the collar? The thought of this almost made
him absent-minded. Once, in copying a letter, he
nearly made a mistake, so that he exclaimed almost
aloud, "Ugh!" and crossed himself. Once in the course
of every month he had a conference with Petrovitch

on the subject of the cloak, where it would be better to buy the cloth, and the color, and the price. He always returned home satisfied, tho troubled, reflecting that the time would come at last when it could all be bought, and then the cloak made.

The affair progressed more briskly than he had expected. Far beyond all his hopes, the director awarded neither forty nor forty-five rubles for Akakiy Akakievitch's share, but sixty. Whether he suspected that Akakiy Akakievitch needed a cloak, or whether it was merely chance, at all events, twenty extra rubles were by this means provided. This circumstance hastened matters. Two or three months more of hunger and Akakiy Akakievitch had accumulated about eighty rubles. His heart, generally so quiet, began to throb. On the first possible day he went shopping in company with Petrovitch. They bought some very good cloth, and at a reasonable rate too, for they had been considering the matter for six months, and rarely let a month pass without their visiting the shops to inquire prices. Petrovitch himself said that no better cloth could be had. For lining, they selected a cotton stuff, but so firm and thick that Petrovitch declared it to be better than silk, and even prettier and more glossy. They did not buy the marten fur because it was, in fact, dear, but in its stead they picked out the very best of cat-skin which could be found in the shop, and which might, indeed, be taken for marten at a distance.

Petrovitch worked at the cloak two whole weeks, for there was a great deal of quilting; otherwise it would have been finished sooner. He charged twelve rubles for the job; it could not possibly have been done for less. It was all sewed with silk, in small,

double seams; and Petrovitch went over each seam
afterward with his own teeth.

It was—it is difficult to say precisely on what day,
but probably the most glorious one in Akakiy Akakievitch's life, when Petrovitch at length brought home
the cloak. He brought it in the morning, before the
hour when it was necessary to start for the department.
Never did a cloak arrive so exactly in the nick of
time, for the severe cold had set in, and it seemed to
threaten to increase. Petrovitch brought the cloak
himself as befits a good tailor. On his countenance
was a significant expression, such as Akakiy Akakievitch had never beheld there. He seemed fully sensi-
ble that he had done no small deed, and crossed a gulf
separating tailors who only put in linings and execute
repairs from those who make new things. He took
the cloak out of the pocket-handkerchief in which he
had brought it. The handkerchief was fresh from the
laundress, and he put it in his pocket for use. Taking
out the cloak, he gazed proudly at it, held it up with
both hands, and flung it skilfully over the shoulders
of Akakiy Akakievitch. Then he pulled it and fitted
it down behind with his hand, and he draped it around
Akakiy Akakievitch without buttoning it. Akakiy
Akakievitch, like an experienced man, wished to try
the sleeves. Petrovitch helped him on with them, and
it turned out that the sleeves were satisfactory also. In
short, the cloak appeared to be perfect and most sea-
sonable. Petrovitch did not neglect to observe that
it was only because he lived in a narrow street, and
had no signboard, and had known Akakiy Akakievitch
so long, that he had made it so cheaply; but that if
he had been in business on the Nevsky Prospect he
would have charged seventy-five rubles for the making

alone. Akakiy Akakievitch did not care to argue this point with Petrovitch. He paid him, thanked him, and set out at once in his new cloak for the department. Petrovitch followed him, and, pausing in the street, gazed long at the cloak in the distance, after which he went to one side expressly to run through a crooked alley and emerge again into the street beyond to gaze once more upon the cloak from another point, namely, directly in front.

Meantime Akakiy Akakievitch went on in holiday mood. He was conscious, every second of the time, that he had a new cloak on his shoulders; and several times he laughed with internal satisfaction. In fact, there were two advantages, one was its warmth, the other its beauty. He saw nothing of the road, but suddenly found himself at the department. He took off his cloak in the anteroom, looked it over carefully, and confided it to the especial care of the attendant. It is impossible to say precisely how it was that every one in the department knew at once that Akakiy Aka-kievitch had a new cloak, and that the "cape" no longer existed. All rushed at the same moment into the anteroom, to inspect it. They congratulated him and said pleasant things to him, so that he began at first to smile and then to grow ashamed. When all surrounded him and said that the new cloak must be "christened," and that he must give a whole evening at least to this, Akakiy Akakievitch lost his head com-pletely, and did not know where he stood, what to answer, or how to get out of it. He stood blushing all over for several minutes, and was on the point of assuring them with great simplicity that it was not a new cloak, that it was so and so, that it was in fact the old "cape."

At length one of the officials, a subchief probably, in order to show that he was not at all proud, and on good terms with his inferiors, said: "So be it, only I will give the party instead of Akakiy Akakievitch; I invite you all to tea with me to-night; it happens quite *à propos*, as it is my name-day." The officials naturally at once offered the subchief their congratulations, and accepted the invitation with pleasure. Akakiy Akakievitch would have declined, but all declared that it was discourteous, that it was simply a sin and a shame, and that he could not possibly refuse. Besides, the notion became pleasant to him when he recollected that he should thereby have a chance of wearing his new cloak in the evening also.

That whole day was truly a most triumphant festival day for Akakiy Akakievitch. He returned home in the most happy frame of mind, took off his cloak, and hung it carefully on the wall, admiring afresh the cloth and the lining. Then he brought out his old, worn-out cloak for comparison. He looked at it and laughed, so vast was the difference. And long after dinner he laughed again when the condition of the "cape" recurred to his mind. He dined cheerfully, and after dinner wrote nothing, but took his ease for a while on the bed, until it got dark. Then he dressed himself leisurely, put on his cloak, and stepped out into the street. Where the host lived, unfortunately, we can not say; our memory begins to fail us badly; and the houses and streets in St. Petersburg have become so mixed up in our head that it is very difficult to get anything out of it again in proper form. This much is certain, that the official lived in the best part of the city; and, therefore, it must have been anything but near to Akakiy Akakievitch's residence. Akakiy

Akakievitch was first obliged to traverse a kind of wilderness of deserted, dimly lighted streets; but in proportion as he approached the official's quarter of the city the streets became more lively, more populous, and more brilliantly illuminated. Pedestrians began to appear; handsomely dressed ladies were more frequently encountered; the men had otter-skin collars to their coats; peasant wagoners, with their gratelike sledges stuck over with brass-headed nails, became rarer; while, on the other hand, more and more drivers in red velvet caps, lacquered sledges, and bear-skin coats began to appear, and carriages with rich hammer-cloths flew swiftly through the streets, their wheels crunching the snow. Akakiy Akakievitch gazed upon all this as upon a novel sight. He had not been in the streets during the evening for years. He halted out of curiosity before a shop-window, to look at a picture representing a handsome woman, who had thrown off her shoe, thereby baring her whole foot in a very pretty way; while behind her the head of a man with whiskers and a handsome mustache peeped through the doorway of another room. Akakiy Akakievitch shook his head and laughed and then went on his way. Why did he laugh? Either because he had met with a thing utterly unknown, but for which every one cherishes, nevertheless, some sort of feeling; or else he thought, like many officials, as follows: "Well, those French! What is to be said? If they do go in anything of that sort, why—" But possibly he did not think at all.

Akakiy Akakievitch at length reached the house in which the subchief lodged. The subchief lived in fine style; the staircase was lit by a lamp, his apartment being on the second floor. On entering the vestibule, Akakiy Akakievitch beheld a whole row of goloshes on the floor. Among them, in the center of the room, stood a samovar, or tea-urn, humming and emitting clouds of steam. On the walls hung all sorts of coats and cloaks, among which there were even some with beaver collars or velvet facings. Beyond, the buzz of conversation was audible, and became clear and loud when the servant came out with a trayful of empty glasses, cream-jugs, and sugar-bowls. It was evident that the officials had arrived long before, and had already finished their first glass of tea.

Akakiy Akakievitch, having hung up his own cloak, entered the inner room. Before him all at once appeared lights, officials, pipes, and card-tables; and he was bewildered by a sound of rapid conversation rising from all the tables, and the noise of moving chairs. He halted very awkwardly in the middle of the room, wondering what he ought to do. But they had seen him. They received him with a shout, and all thronged at once into the anteroom, and there took another look at his cloak. Akakiy Akakievitch, altho somewhat confused, was frank-hearted, and could not refrain from rejoicing when he saw how they praised his cloak. Then, of course, they all dropped him and his cloak, and returned, as was proper, to the tables set out for whist.

All this, the noise, the talk, and the throng of people was rather overwhelming to Akakiy Akakievitch. He simply did not know where he stood, or where to put his hands, his feet, and his whole body. Finally he sat down by the players, looked at the cards, gazed at the face of one and another, and after a while began to gape, and to feel that it was wearisome, the more so as the hour was already long past when he usually went to bed. He wanted to take leave of

the host; but they would not let him go, saying that
he must not fail to drink a glass of champagne, in
honor of his new garment. In the course of an hour,
supper, consisting of vegetables, salad, cold veal, pas-
try, confectioner's pies, and champagne, was served.
They made Akakiy Akakievitch drink two glasses of
champagne, after which he felt things grow livelier.

Still, he could not forget that it was twelve o'clock,
and that he should have been at home long ago. In
order that the host might not think of some excuse
for detaining him, he stole out of the room quickly,
sought out, in the anteroom, his cloak, which, to his
sorrow, he found lying on the floor, brushed it, picked
off every speck upon it, put it on his shoulders, and
descended the stairs to the street.

In the street all was still bright. Some petty shops,
those permanent clubs of servants and all sorts of
folks, were open. Others were shut, but, nevertheless,
showed a streak of light the whole length of the door-
crack, indicating that they were not yet free of company, and that probably some domestics, male and
female, were finishing their stories and conversations,
while leaving their masters in complete ignorance as
to their whereabouts. Akakiy Akakievitch went on in
a happy frame of mind: he even started to run, without knowing why, after some lady, who flew past like
a flash of lightning. But he stopped short, and went
on very quietly as before, wondering why he had quick-
ened his pace. Soon there spread before him those
deserted streets, which are not cheerful in the daytime,
to say nothing of the evening. Now they were even
more dim and lonely: the lanterns began to grow
rarer, oil, evidently, had been less liberally supplied.
Then came wooden houses and fences: not a soul any-

where; only the snow sparkled in the streets and mournfully veiled the low-roofed cabins with their closed shutters. He approached the spot where the street crossed a vast square with houses barely visible on its farther side, a square which seemed a fearful desert.

Afar, a tiny spark glimmered from some watchman's box, which seemed to stand on the edge of the world. Akakiy Akakievitch's cheerfulness diminished at this point in a marked degree. He entered the square, not without an involuntary sensation of fear, as tho his heart warned him of some evil. He glanced back and on both sides, it was like a sea about him. "No, it is better not to look," he thought, and went on, closing his eyes. When he opened them, to see whether he was near the end of the square, he suddenly beheld, standing just before his very nose, some bearded individuals of precisely what sort he could not make out. All grew dark before his eyes, and his heart throbbed.

"But, of course, the cloak is mine!" said one of them in a loud voice, seizing hold of his collar. Akakiy Akakievitch was about to shout "watch" when the second man thrust a fist about the size of a man's head into his mouth, muttering, "Now scream!"

Akakiy Akakievitch felt them strip off his cloak and give him a push with a knee; he fell headlong upon the snow, and felt no more. In a few minutes he recovered consciousness, and rose to his feet; but no one was there. He felt that it was cold in the square and that his cloak was gone; he began to shout, but his voice did not appear to reach to the outskirts of the square. In despair, but without ceasing to shout, he started at a run across the square, straight toward the watch-box, beside which stood the watchman, lean-

ing on his halberd, and apparently curious to know
what kind of a customer was running toward him and
shouting. Akakiy Akakievitch ran up to him, and
began in a sobbing voice to shout that he was asleep
and attended to nothing, and did not see when a man
was robbed. The watch replied that he had seen two
men stop him in the middle of the square, but supposed that they were friends of his; and that, instead
of scolding vainly, he had better go to the police on
the morrow, so that they might make a search for
whoever had stolen the cloak.

Akakiy Akakievitch ran home in complete disorder;
his hair, which grew very thinly upon his temples and
the back of his head, wholly disordered; his body,
arms, and legs covered with snow. The old woman,
who was mistress of his lodgings, on hearing a terrible
knocking, sprang hastily from her bed, and, with only
one shoe on, ran to open the door, pressing the sleeve
of her chemise to her bosom out of modesty; but when
she had opened it she fell back on beholding Akakiy
Akakievitch in such a state. When he told her about
the affair she clasped her hands, and said that he must
go straight to the district chief of police, for his sub-
ordinate would turn up his nose, promise well, and
drop the matter there. The very best thing to do,
therefore, would be to go to the district chief, whom
she knew, because Finnish Anna, her former cook,
was now nurse at his house. She often saw him passing
the house; and he was at church every Sunday, praying, but at the same time gazing cheerfully at everybody; so that he must be a good man, judging from
all appearances. Having listened to this opinion,
Akakiy Akakievitch betook himself sadly to his room:

and how he spent the night there any one who can
put himself in another's place may readily imagine.

Early in the morning he presented himself at the
district chief's; but was told that this official was
asleep. He went again at ten and was again informed
that he was asleep; at eleven, and they said, "The
superintendent is not at home"; at dinner time, and
the clerks in the anteroom would not admit him on any
terms, and insisted upon knowing his business. So
that at last, for once in his life, Akakiy Akakievitch
felt an inclination to show some spirit, and said curtly
that he must see the chief in person; that they ought
not to presume to refuse him entrance; that he came
from the department of justice, and that when he com-
plained of them, they would see.

The clerks dared make no reply to this, and one of
them went to call the chief, who listened to the strange
story of the theft of the coat. Instead of directing
his attention to the principal points of the matter, he
began to question Akakiy Akakievitch: Why was he
going home so late? Was he in the habit of doing so,
or had he been to some disorderly house? So that
Akakiy Akakievitch got thoroughly confused, and left
him without knowing whether the affair of his cloak
was in proper train or not.

All that day, for the first time in his life, he never
went near the department. The next day he made his
appearance, very pale, and in his old cape, which had
become even more shabby. The news of the robbery
of the cloak touched many; altho there were some
officials present who never lost an opportunity, even
such a one as the present, of ridiculing Akakiy Akakievitch. They decided to make a collection for him
on the spot, but the officials had already spent a great

deal in subscribing for the director's portrait, and for
some book, at the suggestion of the head of that division, who was a friend of the author; and so the sum
was trifling.

One of them, moved by pity, resolved to help Akakiy
Akakievitch with some good advice at least, and told
him that he ought not to go to the police, for altho
it might happen that a police officer, wishing to win
the approval of his superiors, might hunt up the cloak
by some means, still his cloak would remain in the
possession of the police if he did not offer legal proof
that it belonged to him. The best thing for him,
therefore, would be to apply to a certain prominent
personage; since this prominent personage, by entering
into relations with the proper persons, could greatly
expedite the matter.

As there was nothing else to be done, Akakiy Akakievitch decided to go to the prominent personage.
What was the exact official position of the prominent
personage remains unknown to this day. The reader
must know that the prominent personage had but
recently become a prominent personage, having up to
that time been only an insignificant person. Moreover,
his present position was not considered prominent in
comparison with others still more so. But there is
always a circle of people to whom what is insignificant
in the eyes of others is important enough. Moreover,
he strove to increase his importance by sundry devices;
for instance, he managed to have the inferior officials
meet him on the staircase when he entered upon his
service; no one was to presume to come directly to
him, but the strictest etiquette must be observed; the
collegiate recorder must make a report to the government secretary, the government secretary to the titular

councilor, or whatever other man was proper, and all business must come before him in this manner. In Holy Russia all is thus contaminated with the love of imitation; every man imitates and copies his superior. They even say that a certain titular councilor, when promoted to the head of some small separate room, immediately partitioned off a private room for himself, called it the audience chamber, and posted at the door a lackey with red collar and braid, who grasped the handle of the door and opened to all comers; tho the audience chamber would hardly hold an ordinary writing table.

The manners and customs of the prominent personage were grand and imposing, but rather exaggerated. The main foundation of his system was strictness. "Strictness, strictness, and always strictness!" he generally said; and at the last word he looked significantly into the face of the person to whom he spoke. But there was no necessity for this, for the half-score of subordinates, who formed the entire force of the office, were properly afraid; on catching sight of him afar off, they left their work, and waited, drawn up in line, until he had passed through the room. His ordinary converse with his inferiors smacked of sternness, and consisted chiefly of three phrases: "How dare you?" "Do you know whom you are speaking to?" "Do you realize who stands before you?"

Otherwise he was a very kind-hearted man, good to his comrades, and ready to oblige; but the rank of general threw him completely off his balance. On receiving any one of that rank he became confused, lost his way, as it were, and never knew what to do. If he chanced to be among his equals, he was still a very nice kind of man, a very good fellow in many respects, and not stupid; but the very moment that he found himself in the society of people but one rank lower than himself, he became silent; and his situation aroused sympathy, the more so as he felt himself that he might have been making an incomparably better use of his time. In his eyes there was sometimes visible a desire to join some interesting conversation or group; but he was kept back by the thought, "Would it not be a very great condescension on his part? Would it not be familiar? and would he not thereby lose his importance?" And in consequence of such reflections he always remained in the same dumb state, uttering from time to time a few monosyllabic sounds, and thereby earning the name of the most wearisome of men.

To this prominent personage, Akakiy Akakievitch presented himself, and this at the most unfavorable time for himself, tho opportune for the prominent personage. The prominent personage was in his cabinet, conversing very gaily with an old acquaintance and companion of his childhood, whom he had not seen for several years, and who had just arrived, when it was announced to him that a person named Bashmatchkin had come. He asked abruptly: "Who is he?" "Some official," he was informed. "Ah, he can wait! this is no time for him to call," said the important man.

It must be remarked here that the important man lied outrageously: he had said all he had to say to his friend long before; and the conversation had been interspersed for some time with very long pauses, during which they merely slapped each other on the leg, and said: "You think so, Ivan Abramovitch?"

"Just so, Stephen Varlamovitch!" Nevertheless, he ordered that the official should be kept waiting, in order to show his friend, a man who had not been in the service for a long time, but had lived at home in the country, how long officials had to wait in his anteroom.

At length, having talked himself completely out, and more than that, having had his fill of pauses, and smoked a cigar in a very comfortable armchair with reclining back, he suddenly seemed to recollect, and said to the secretary, who stood by the door with papers of reports, "So it seems that there is a tchinovnik waiting to see me. Tell him that he may come in." On perceiving Akakiy Akakievitch's modest mien and his worn undress uniform, he turned abruptly to him and said: "What do you want?" in a curt, hard voice, which he had practised in his room in private, and before the looking-glass, for a whole week before being raised to his present rank.

Akakiy Akakievitch, who was already imbued with a due amount of fear, became somewhat confused; and, as well as his tongue would permit, explained, with a rather more frequent addition than usual of the word "that," that his cloak was quite new and had been stolen in the most inhuman manner; that he had applied to him in order that he might, in some way, by his intermediation—that he might enter into correspondence with the chief of police, and find the cloak.

For some inexplicable reason this conduct seemed familiar to the prominent personage. "What, my dear sir!" he said abruptly, "are you not acquainted with etiquette? Where have you come from? Don't you know how such matters are managed? You should first have entered a complaint about this at the court below: it would have gone to the head of the department, then to the chief of the division, then it would have been handed over to the secretary, and the secretary would have given it to me."

"But, your excellency," said Akakiy Akakievitch, trying to collect his small handful of wits, and conscious at the same time that he was perspiring terribly, "I, your excellency, presumed to trouble you because secretaries—are an untrustworthy race."

"What, what, what!" said the important personage. "Where did you get such courage? Where did you get such ideas? What impudence toward their chiefs and superiors has spread among the young generation!" The prominent personage apparently had not observed that Akakiy Akakievitch was already in the neighborhood of fifty. If he could be called a young man, it must have been in comparison with some one who was seventy. "Do you know to whom you speak? Do you realize who stands before you? Do you realize it? do you realize it? I ask you!" Then he stamped his foot and raised his voice to such a pitch that it would have frightened even a different man from Akakiy Akakievitch.

Akakiy Akakievitch's senses failed him; he staggered, trembled in every limb, and, if the porters had not run in to support him, would have fallen to the floor. They carried him out insensible. But the prominent personage, gratified that the effect should have surpassed his expectations, and quite intoxicated with the thought that his word could even deprive a man of his senses, glanced sidewise at his friend in order to see how he looked upon this, and perceived, not without satisfaction, that his friend was in a most uneasy frame of mind, and even beginning, on his part, to feel a trifle frightened.

Akakiy Akakievitch could not remember how he descended the stairs, and got into the street. He felt neither his hands nor feet. Never in his life had he been so rated by any high official, let alone a strange one. He went staggering on through the snowstorm, which was blowing in the streets, with his mouth wide open; the wind, in St. Petersburg fashion, darted upon him from all quarters, and down every cross street. In a twinkling it had blown a quinsy into his throat, and he reached home unable to utter a word. His throat was swollen, and he lay down on his bed. So powerful is sometimes a good scolding!

The next day a violent fever showed itself. Thanks to the generous assistance of the St. Petersburg climate, the malady progressed more rapidly than could have been expected; and when the doctor arrived, he found, on feeling the sick man's pulse, that there was nothing to be done, except to prescribe a fomentation, so that the patient might not be left entirely without the beneficent aid of medicine; but at the same time he predicted his end in thirty-six hours. After this he turned to the landlady, and said: "And as for you, don't waste your time on him: order his pine coffin now, for an oak one will be too expensive for him." Did Akakiy Akakievitch hear these fatal words? and if he heard them, did they produce any overwhelming effect upon him? Did he lament the bitterness of his life? We know not, for he continued in a delirious condition. Visions incessantly appeared to him, each stranger than the other. Now he saw Petrovitch and ordered him to make a cloak with some traps for robbers who seemed to him to be always under the bed;

and cried every moment to the landlady to pull one
of them from under his coverlet. Then he inquired
why his old mantle hung before him when he had a
new cloak. Next he fancied that he was standing
before the prominent person listening to a thorough
setting-down and saying: "Forgive me, your excellency!" but at last he began to curse, uttering the
most horrible words, so that his aged landlady crossed
herself, never in her life having heard anything of the
kind from him, the more so, as those words followed
directly after the words "your excellency." Later on
he talked utter nonsense, of which nothing could be
made: all that was evident being that his incoherent
words and thoughts hovered ever about one thing, his
cloak.

At length poor Akakiy Akakievitch breathed his last.
They sealed up neither his room nor his effects,
because, in the first place, there were no heirs, and,
in the second, there was very little to inherit beyond
a bundle of goose-quills, a quire of white official paper,
three pairs of socks, two or three buttons which had
burst off his trousers, and the mantle already known
to the reader. To whom all this fell, God knows. I
confess that the person who told me this tale took no
interest in the matter. They carried Akakiy Akakievitch out, and buried him.

And St. Petersburg was left without Akakiy Akakievitch, as tho he had never lived there. A being
disappeared, who was protected by none, dear to none,
interesting to none, and who never even attracted to
himself the attention of those students of human
nature, who omit no opportunity of thrusting a pin
through a common fly, and examining it under the
microscope. A being who bore meekly the jibes of

the department, and went to his grave without having
done one unusual deed, but to whom, nevertheless, at
the close of his life, appeared a bright visitant in the
form of a cloak, which momentarily cheered his poor
life, and upon whom, thereafter, an intolerable misfortune descended, just as it descends upon the heads
of the mighty of this world!

Several days after his death, the porter was sent
from the department to his lodgings with an order
for him to present himself there immediately; the chief
commanding it. But the porter had to return unsuc-
cessful, with the answer that he could not come; and
to the question, "Why?" replied, "Well, because he
is dead! he was buried four days ago." In this manner
did they hear of Akakiy Akakievitch's death at the
department; and the next day a new official sat in his
place, with a handwriting by no means so upright, but
more inclined and slanting.

But who could have imagined that this was not
really the end of Akakiy Akakievitch, that he was
destined to raise a commotion after death, as if in
compensation for his utterly insignificant life? But
so it happened, and our poor story unexpectedly gains
a fantastic ending.

A rumor suddenly spread through St. Petersburg
that a dead man had taken to appearing on the Kalinkin Bridge and its vicinity, at night, in the form of a
tchinovnik seeking a stolen cloak, and that, under the
pretext of its being the stolen cloak, he dragged, without regard to rank or calling, every one's cloak from
his shoulders, be it catskin, beaver, fox, bear, sable;
in a word, every sort of fur and skin which men
adopted for their covering. One of the department
officials saw the dead man with his own eyes, and

immediately recognized in him Akakiy Akakievitch. This, however, inspired him with such terror that he ran off with all his might, and therefore did not scan the dead man closely, but only saw how the latter threatened him from afar with his finger. Constant complaints poured in from all quarters, of those who were exposed to the danger of a cold, on account of the frequent dragging off of their cloaks.

Arrangements were made by the police to catch the corpse, alive or dead, at any cost, and punish him as an example to others, in the most severe manner. In this they nearly succeeded; for a watchman, on guard in Kirushkin Alley, caught the corpse by the collar on the very scene of his evil deeds, when attempting to pull off the frieze cloak of a retired musician. Having seized him by the collar, he summoned, with a shout, two of his comrades, whom he enjoined to hold him fast, while he himself felt for a moment in his boot, in order to draw out his snuff-box, and refresh his frozen nose. But the snuff was of a sort which even a corpse could not endure. The watchman, having closed his right nostril with his finger, had no sooner succeeded in holding half a handful up to the left than the corpse sneezed so violently that he completely filled the eyes of all three. While they raised their hands to wipe them, the dead man vanished completely, so that they positively did not know whether they had actually had him in their grip at all. Thereafter the watchmen conceived such a terror of dead men that they were afraid even to seize the living, and only screamed from a distance: "Hey, there! go your way!" So the dead tchinovnik began to appear, even beyond the Kalinkin Bridge, causing no little terror to all timid people.

But we have totally neglected that certain prominent personage, who may really be considered as the cause of the fantastic turn taken by this true history. First of all, justice compels us to say that after the departure of poor, annihilated Akakiy Akakievitch, he felt something like remorse. Suffering was unpleasant to him, for his heart was accessible to many good impulses, in spite of the fact that his rank often prevented his showing his true self. As soon as his friend had left his cabinet he began to think about poor Akakiy Akakievitch. And from that day forth poor Akakiy Akakievitch, who could not bear up under an official reprimand, recurred to his mind almost every day. The thought troubled him to such an extent that a week later he even resolved to send an official to him, to learn whether he really could assist him; and when it was reported to him that Akakiy Akakievitch had died suddenly of fever, he was startled, harkened to the reproaches of his conscience, and was out of sorts for the whole day.

Wishing to divert his mind in some way, and drive away the disagreeable impression, he set out that evening for one of his friends' houses, where he found quite a large party assembled. What was better, nearly every one was of the same rank as himself, so that he need not feel in the least constrained. This had a marvelous effect upon his mental state. He grew expansive, made himself agreeable in conversation, in short, he passed a delightful evening. After supper he drank a couple of glasses of champagne—not a bad recipe for cheerfulness, as every one knows. The champagne inclined him to various adventures; and he determined not to return home, but to go and see a certain well-known lady, of German extraction, Karo-

lina Ivanovna, a lady, it appears, with whom he was
on a very friendly footing.

It must be mentioned that the prominent personage
was no longer a young man, but a good husband, and
respected father of a family. Two sons, one of whom
was already in the service; and a good-looking, sixteen-
year-old daughter, with a rather *retroussé* but pretty
little nose, came every morning to kiss his hand, and
say: "*Bon jour*, papa." His wife, a still fresh and
good-looking woman, first gave him her hand to kiss,
and then, reversing the procedure, kissed his. But
the prominent personage, tho perfectly satisfied in
his domestic relations, considered it stylish to have a
friend in another quarter of the city. This friend was
scarcely prettier or younger than his wife; but there
are such puzzles in the world, and it is not our place
to judge them. So the important personage descended
the stairs, stepped into his sledge, said to the coachman, "To Karolina Ivanovna's," and, wrapping himself luxuriously in his warm cloak, found himself in
that delightful frame of mind than which a Russian
can conceive nothing better, namely, when you think
of nothing yourself, yet when the thoughts creep into
your mind of their own accord, each more agreeable
than the other, giving you no trouble either to drive
them away or seek them. Fully satisfied, he recalled
all the gay features of the evening just passed, and all
the *mots* which had made the little circle laugh. Many
of them he repeated in a low voice, and found them
quite as funny as before; so it is not surprising that he
should laugh heartily at them. Occasionally, however, he was interrupted by gusts of wind, which, coming suddenly, God knows whence or why, cut his
face, drove masses of snow into it, filled out his cloak-

collar like a sail, or suddenly blew it over his head
with supernatural force, and thus caused him constant
trouble to disentangle himself.

Suddenly the important personage felt some one
clutch him firmly by the collar. Turning round, he
perceived a man of short stature, in an old, worn,
uniform, and recognized, not without terror, Akakiy
Akakievitch. The official's face was white as snow,
and looked just like a corpse's. But the horror of the
important personage transcended all bounds when he
saw the dead man's mouth open, and, with a terrible
odor of the grave, give vent to the following remarks:
"Ah, here you are at last! I have you, that—by the
collar! I need your cloak; you took no trouble about
mine, but reprimanded me; so now give up your own."

The pallid prominent personage almost died of
fright. Brave as he was in the office and in the presence of inferiors generally, and altho, at the sight
of his manly form and appearance, every one said,
"Ugh! how much character he has!" at this crisis, he,
like many possessed of a heroic exterior, experienced
such terror that, not without cause, he began to fear
an attack of illness. He flung his cloak hastily from
his shoulders and shouted to his coachman in an unnatural voice: "Home at full speed." The coachman,
hearing the tone which is generally employed at critical
moments, and even accompanied by something much
more tangible, drew his head down between his shoulders in case of an emergency, flourished his whip, and
flew on like an arrow. In a little more than six minutes the prominent personage was at the entrance of
his own house. Pale, thoroughly scared, and cloak-
less, he went home instead of to Karolina Ivanovna's,
reached his room somehow or other, and passed the

night in the direst distress; so that the next morning over their tea his daughter said: "You are very pale to-day, papa." But papa remained silent, and said not a word to any one of what had happened to him, where he had been, or where he had intended to go.

This occurrence made a deep impression upon him. He even began to say: "How dare you? do you realize who stands before you?" less frequently to the under-officials, and, if he did utter the words, it was only after first having learned the bearings of the matter. But the most noteworthy point was that from that day forward the apparition of the dead tchinovnik ceased to be seen. Evidently the prominent personage's cloak just fitted his shoulders; at all events, no more instances of his dragging cloaks from people's shoulders were heard of. But many active and apprehensive persons could by no means reassure themselves, and asserted that the dead tchinovnik still showed himself in distant parts of the city.

In fact, one watchman in Kolomna saw with his own eyes the apparition come from behind a house. But being rather weak of body, he dared not arrest him, but followed him in the dark, until, at length, the apparition looked round, paused, and inquired: "What do you want?" at the same time showing such a fist as is never seen on living men. The watchman said: "It's of no consequence," and turned back instantly. But the apparition was much too tall, wore huge mustaches, and, directing its steps apparently toward the Obukhoff Bridge, disappeared in the darkness of the night.

FAME'S LITTLE DAY

By Sarah Orne Jewett

Chapter I

Nobody ever knew, except himself, what made a
foolish young newspaper reporter, who happened into
a small old-fashioned hotel in New York, observe
Mr. Abel Pinkham with deep interest, listen to his
talk, ask a question or two of the clerk, and then go
away and make up an effective personal paragraph
for one of the morning papers. He must have had a
heart full of fun, this young reporter, and something
honestly rustic and pleasing must have struck him in
the guest's demeanor, for there was a flavor in the few
lines he wrote that made some of his fellows seize upon
the little paragraph, and copy it, and add to it, and
keep it moving. Nobody knows what starts such a
thing in journalism, or keeps it alive after it is started,
but on a certain Thursday morning the fact was made
known to the world that among the notabilities then
in the city, Abel Pinkham, Esquire, a distinguished citizen of Wetherford, Vermont, was visiting New York
on important affairs connected with the maple-sugar
industry of his native State. Mr. Pinkham had expected to keep his visit unannounced, but it was likely
to occasion much interest in business and civic circles.
This was something like the way that the paragraph

(Used by permission of and by arrangement with Houghton
Mifflin Co.)

started; but here and there a kindred spirit of the original journalist caught it up and added discreet lines about Mr. Pinkham's probable stay in town, his occupation of an apartment on the fourth floor of the Ethan Allen Hotel, and other circumstances so uninteresting to the reading public in general that presently in the next evening edition, one city editor after another threw out the item, and the young journalists, having had their day of pleasure, passed on to other things.

Mr. and Mrs. Pinkham had set forth from home with many forebodings, in spite of having talked all winter about taking this journey as soon as the spring opened. They would have caught at any reasonable excuse for giving it up altogether, because when the time arrived it seemed so much easier to stay at home. Mrs. Abel Pinkham had never seen New York; her husband himself had not been to the city for a great many years; in fact, his reminiscences of the former visit were not altogether pleasant, since he had foolishly fallen into many snares, and been much gulled in his character of honest young countryman. There was a tarnished and worthless counterfeit of a large gold watch still concealed between the outer boarding and inner lath and plaster of the lean-to bedroom which Mr. Abel Pinkham had occupied as a bachelor; it was not the only witness of his being taken in by city sharpers, and he had winced ever since at the thought of their wiles. But he was now a man of sixty, well-to-do, and of authority in town affairs; his children were all well married and settled in homes of their own, except a widowed daughter, who lived at home with her young son, and was her mother's lieutenant in household affairs.

The boy was almost grown, and at this season, when the maple sugar was all made and shipped, and it was still too early for spring work on the land, Mr. Pinkham could leave home as well as not, and here he was in New York, feeling himself to be a stranger and foreigner to city ways. If it had not been for that desire to appear well in his wife's eyes, which had buoyed him over the bar of many difficulties, he could have found it in his heart to take the next train back to Wetherford, Vermont, to be there rid of his best clothes and the stiff rim of his heavy felt hat. He could not let his wife discover that the noise and confusion of Broadway had the least power to make him flinch: he cared no more for it than for the woods in snow-time. He was as good as anybody, and she was better. They owed nobody a cent; and they had come on purpose to see the city of New York.

They were sitting at the breakfast-table in the Ethan Allen Hotel, having arrived at nightfall the day before. Mrs. Pinkham looked a little pale about the mouth. She had been kept awake nearly all night by the noise, and had enjoyed but little the evening she had spent in the stuffy parlor of the hotel, looking down out of the window at what seemed to her but garish scenes, and keeping a reproachful and suspicious eye upon some unpleasantly noisy young women of forward behavior who were her only companions. Abel himself was by no means so poorly entertained in the hotel office and smoking-room. He felt much more at home than she did, being better used to meeting strange men than she was to strange women, and he found two or three companions who had seen more than he of New York life. It was there, indeed, that the young reporter found him, hearty and country-fed, and loved the appearance of his best clothes, and the way Mr. Abel Pinkham brushed his hair, and loved the way that he spoke in a loud and manful voice the belief and experience of his honest heart.

In the morning at breakfast-time the Pinkhams were depressed. They missed their good bed at home; they were troubled by the roar and noise of the streets that hardly stopped over night before it began again in the morning. The waiter did not put what mind he may have had to the business of serving them; and Mrs. Abel Pinkham, whose cooking was the triumph of parish festivals at home, had her own opinion about the beefsteak. She was a woman of imagination, and now that she was fairly here, spectacles and all, it really pained her to find that the New York of her dreams, the metropolis of dignity and distinction, of wealth and elegance, did not seem to exist. These poor streets, these unlovely people, were the end of a great illusion. They did not like to meet each other's eyes, this worthy pair. The man began to put on an unbecoming air of assertion, and Mrs. Pinkham's face was full of lofty protest.

"My gracious me, Mary Ann! I *am* glad I happened to get the 'Tribune' this mornin'," said Mr. Pinkham, with sudden excitement. "Just you look here! I'd like well to know how they found out about our comin'!" and he handed the paper to his wife across the table. There—there 't is; right by my thumb," he insisted. "Can't you see it?" and he smiled like a boy as she finally brought her large spectacles to bear upon the important paragraph.

"I guess they think somethin' of us, if you don't think much o' them," continued Mr. Pinkham, grandly. "Oh, they know how to keep the run o' folks who are somebody to home! Draper and Fitch knew we was comin' this week: you know I sent word I was comin' to settle with them myself. I suppose they send folks round to the hotels, these newspapers, but I shouldn't thought there'd been time. Anyway, they've thought 't was worth while to put us in!"

Mrs. Pinkham did not take the trouble to make a mystery out of the unexpected pleasure. "I want to cut it out an' send it right up home to daughter Sarah," she said, beaming with pride, and looking at the printed names as if they were flattering photographs. "I think 't was most too strong to say we was among the notables. But there! 't is their business to dress up things, and they have to print somethin' every day. I guess I shall go up and put on my best dress," she added, inconsequently; "this one's kind of dusty; it's the same I rode in."

"Le' me see that paper again," said Mr. Pinkham jealously. "I didn't more 'n half sense it, I was so taken aback. Well, Mary Ann, you didn't expect you was goin' to get into the papers when you came away. '*Abel Pinkham, Esquire, of Wetherford, Vermont.*' It looks well, don't it? But you might have knocked me down with a feather when I first caught sight of them words."

"I guess I shall put on my other dress," said Mrs. Pinkham, rising, with quite a different air from that with which she had sat down to her morning meal. "This one looks a little out o' style, as Sarah said, but when I got up this mornin' I was so homesick it didn't seem to make any kind o' difference. I expect that saucy girl last night took us to be nobodies. I'd like to leave the paper round where she couldn't help seein' it."

"Don't take any notice of her," said Abel, in a dig-

nified tone. "If she can't do what you want an' be
civil, we'll go somewheres else. I wish I'd done what
we talked of at first an' gone to the Astor House,
but that young man in the cars told me 't was remote
from the things we should want to see. The Astor
House was the top o' everything when I was here last,
but I expected to find some changes. I want you to
have the best there is," he said, smiling at his wife as
if they were just making their wedding journey.
"Come, let's be stirrin'; 't is long past eight o'clock,"
and he ushered her to the door, newspaper in hand.

Chapter II

Later that day the guests walked up Broadway,
holding themselves erect, and feeling as if every eye
was upon them. Abel Pinkham had settled with his
correspondents for the spring consignments of maple
sugar, and a round sum in bank bills was stowed away
in his breast pocket. One of the partners had been
a Wetherford boy, so when there came a renewal of
interest in maple sugar, and the best confectioners were
ready to do it honor, the finest quality being at a large
premium, this partner remembered that there never
was any sugar made in Wetherford of such melting and
delicious flavor as from the trees on the old Pinkham
farm. He had now made a good bit of money for
himself on this private venture, and was ready that
morning to pay Mr. Abel Pinkham cash down, and
to give him a handsome order for the next season for
all he could make. Mr. Fitch was also generous in
the matter of such details as freight and packing; he
was immensely polite and kind to his old friends, and
begged them to come out and stay with him and his

wife, where they lived now, in a not far distant New Jersey town.

"No, no, sir," said Mr. Pinkham promptly. "My wife has come to see the city, and our time is short. Your folks 'll be up this summer, won't they? We'll wait an' visit then."

"You must certainly take Mrs. Pinkham up to the Park," said the commission merchant. "I wish I had time to show you round myself. I suppose you've been seeing some things already, haven't you? I noticed your arrival in the 'Herald.'"

"The 'Tribune' it was," said Mr. Pinkham, blushing through a smile and looking round at his wife.

"Oh no; I never read the 'Tribune,'" said Mr. Fitch. "There was quite an extended notice in my paper. They must have put you and Mrs. Pinkham into the 'Herald' too." And so the friends parted, laughing. "I am much pleased to have a call from such distinguished parties," said Mr. Fitch, by way of final farewell, and Mr. Pinkham waved his hand grandly in reply.

"Let's get the 'Herald,' then," he said, as they started up the street. "We can go an' sit over in that little square that we passed as we came along, and rest an' talk things over about what we'd better do this afternoon. I'm tired out a-trampin' and standin'. I'd rather have set still while we were there, but he wanted us to see his store. Done very well, Joe Fitch has, but 'tain't a business I should like."

There was a lofty look and sense of behavior about Mr. Pinkham of Wetherford. You might have thought him a great politician as he marched up Broadway, looking neither to right hand nor left. He felt himself to be a person of great responsibilities.

"I begin to feel sort of at home myself," said his wife, who always had a certain touch of simple dignity about her. "When we was comin' yesterday New York seemed to be all strange, and there wasn't nobody expectin' us. I feel now just as if I'd been here before."

They were now on the edge of the better-looking part of the town; it was still noisy and crowded, but noisy with fine carriages instead of drays, and crowded with well-dressed people. The hours for shopping and visiting were beginning, and more than one person looked with appreciative and friendly eyes at the comfortable pleased-looking elderly man and woman who went their easily beguiled and loitering way. The pavement peddlers detained them, but the cabmen beckoned them in vain; their eyes were busy with the immediate foreground. Mrs. Pinkham was embarrassed by the recurring reflection of herself in the great windows.

"I wish I had seen about a new bonnet before we came," she lamented. "They seem to be havin' on some o' their spring things."

"Don't you worry, Mary Ann. I don't see anybody that looks any better than you do," said Abel, with boyish and reassuring pride.

Mr. Pinkham had now bought the "Herald," and also the "Sun," well recommended by an able newsboy, and presently they crossed over from that corner by the Fifth Avenue Hotel which seems like the very heart of New York, and found a place to sit down on the Square—an empty bench, where they could sit side by side and look the papers through, reading over each other's shoulder, and being impatient from page to page. The paragraph was indeed repeated, with trifling additions. Ederton of the "Sun" had followed the "Tribune" man's lead, and fabricated a brief interview, a marvel of art and discretion, but so general in its allusions that it could create no suspicion; it almost deceived Mr. Pinkham himself, so that he found unaffected pleasure in the fictitious occasion, and felt as if he had easily covered himself with glory. Except for the bare fact of the interview's being imaginary, there was no discredit to be cast upon Mr. Abel Pinkham's having said that he thought the country near Wetherford looked well for the time of year, and promised a fair hay crop, and that his income was augmented one-half to three-fifths by his belief in the future of maple sugar. It was likely to be the great coming crop of the Green Mountain State. Ederton suggested that there was talk of Mr. Pinkham's presence in the matter of a great maple-sugar trust, in which much of the capital of Wall Street would be involved.

"How they do hatch up these things, don't they?" said the worthy man at this point. "Well, it all sounds well, Mary Ann."

"It says here that you are a very personable man," smiled his wife, "and have filled some of the most responsible town offices" (this was the turn taken by Goffey of the "Herald"). "Oh, and that you are going to attend the performance at Barnum's this evening, and occupy reserved seats. Why, I didn't know—who have you told about that?—who was you talkin to last night, Abel?"

"I never spoke o' goin' to Barnum's to any livin' soul," insisted Abel, flushing. "I only thought of it two or three times to myself that perhaps I might go an' take you. Now that is singular; perhaps they put that in just to advertize the show."

"Ain't it a kind of a low place for folks like us to be seen in?" suggested Mrs. Pinkham timidly. "People seem to be payin' us all this attention, an' I don't know's 't would be dignified for us to go to one o' them circus places."

"I don't care; we shan't live but once. I ain't comin' to New York an' confine myself to evenin' meetin's," answered Abel, throwing away discretion and morality together. "I tell you I'm goin' to spend this sugar-money just as we've a mind to. You've worked hard, an' counted a good while on comin', and so 've I; an' I ain't goin' to mince my steps an' pinch an' screw for nobody. I'm goin' to hire one o' them hacks an' ride up to the Park."

"Joe Fitch said we could go right up in one o' the elevated railroads for five cents, an' return when we was ready," protested Mary Ann, who had a thriftier inclination than her husband; but Mr. Pinkham was not to be let or hindered, and they presently found themselves going up Fifth Avenue in a somewhat battered open landau. The spring sun shone upon them, and the spring breeze fluttered the black ostrich tip on Mrs. Pinkham's durable winter bonnet, and brought the pretty color to her faded cheeks.

"There! this is something like. Such people as we are can't go meechin' round; it ain't expected. Don't it pay for a lot o' hard work?" said Abel; and his wife gave him a pleased look for her only answer. They were both thinking of their gray farm-house high on a long western slope, with the afternoon sun full in its face, the old red barn, the pasture, the shaggy woods that stretched far up the mountain-side.

"I wish Sarah an' little Abel was here to see us ride by," said Mary Ann Pinkham, presently. "I can't seem to wait to have 'em get that newspaper. I'm so glad we sent it right off before we started this mornin'. If Abel goes to the post-office comin' from school, as he always does, they'll have it to read to-morrow before supper-time."

Chapter III

This happy day in two plain lives ended, as might have been expected, with the great Barnum show. Mr. and Mrs. Pinkham found themselves in possession of countless advertizing cards and circulars next morning, and these added somewhat to their sense of responsibility. Mrs. Pinkham became afraid that the hotel-keeper would charge them double. "We've got to pay for it some way; there. I don't know but I'm more'n willin'," said the good soul. "I never did have such a splendid time in all my life. Findin' you so respected 'way off here is the best of anything; an' then seein' them dear little babies in their nice carriages, all along the streets and up to the Central Park! I never shall forget them beautiful little creatur's. And then the houses, an' the hosses, an' the store windows, an' all the rest of it! Well, I can't make any country pitcher hold no more, an' I want to get home an' think it over, goin' about my housework."

They were just entering the door of the Ethan Allen Hotel for the last time, when a young man met them and bowed cordially. He was the original reporter of their arrival, but they did not know it, and the impulse was strong within him to formally invite Mr. Pinkham to make an address before the members of the Produce Exchange on the following morning; but he had been a country boy himself, and their look of seriousness and self-consciousness appealed to him un, expectedly. He wondered what effect this great experience would have upon their after-life. The best fun, after all, would be to send marked copies of his paper and Ederton's to all the weekly newspapers in that part of Vermont. He saw before him the evidence of their happy increase of self-respect, and he would make all their neighborhood agree to do them honor. Such is the dominion of the press.

"Who was that young man?—he kind of bowed to you," asked the lady from Wetherford, after the journalist had meekly passed; but Abel Pinkham, Esquire, could only tell her that he looked like a young fellow who was sitting in the office the evening that they came to the hotel. The reporter did not seem to these distinguished persons to be a young man of any consequence.

A GREAT RUSHING OF WINGS

By Emma-Lindsay Squier

The girl had gone down into the valley of Death.
And she had come back—bringing a new life into the
world. Now she lay quietly, scarcely breathing, her
lips parted in a tired, contented smile. The village
doctor was speaking in a very low voice to the midwife. "—A pity—that fall she had when she learned
of Pierre's death. The little one here—he will never
walk. The legs are paralyzed."

The closed eyes of the girl mother flashed open, big
and dark and filled with tragic pain.

"Monsieur Doctor," she faltered weakly, "—I heard
you say—or perhaps I but dreamed—my baby—he will
be strong, and healthy?"

The doctor turned his honest, embarrassed face
away.

"Oh, to be sure," he mumbled, "he will be strong
enough. Listen to the young rascal trying out his
lungs."

The girl half rose from the bed. "But you said—
you said—"

The midwife pushed her gently back against the pillows. "There, there, little one, do not excite yourself.
Monsieur Doctor—what does the old fool know about
babies? Puh! I was helping to bring babies into the
world when he was spilling soup on his schoolboy
blouse."

But the girl lay back with closed eyes, and great tears welled from beneath the blue-white lids and streaked the pallor of her cheeks. Her lips were trembling.

"Do not trouble to spare me, Mother Boucharde," she whispered. "I dreamed that this thing would be. I dreamed that my baby crawled on the floor, dragged his little helpless limbs, and cried out to me, stretching up his tiny hands. It is my punishment. I loved Pierre too much—more than God!"

The midwife patted her cheek, and smoothed the soft black hair from around her face. "Not so, my little one. Your love for Pierre was beautiful—and his for you. Never let yourself think that the good God would punish one of his children for a holy love like that," she said.

"This misfortune which has come upon you—" the honest doctor, used as he was to scenes of sorrow and bitterness, hesitated, blew his nose and turned away, unable to finish the sentence.

The dark eyes opened wide once more. "Then it *is* true?"

The doctor hesitated, then sighed. "Yes, my little one, I am afraid so."

Pierre *Sans Sou* they had called him, that rollicking, improvident young fiddler who had won the heart of the maid, Jeanette. And now he was gone, thrust violently through Death's door, just when the great joy of parenthood was about to bless their union. Death, as well as Life, had made bitterly truthful the laughing nickname by which the villagers had called Pierre. There was nothing left, not a sou.

Jeanette, with her eyes bigger and darker than ever, and a stillness of mind that was like the paralysis that chained her baby's limbs, went back to the village inn, back to the work from which Pierre had taken her. Madame Luconne had grudgingly given permission for the baby to be kept with Jeanette.

"After all," she said, shrugging her shoulders, "he will not be much in the way, since he has not the use of his limbs." The girl's face grew rigid, and her eyelids fluttered like tortured birds.

"No," she answered, almost in a whisper, "he will not be in the way."

Day by day, month by month, the girl mother lived with her heart upon the rack—day by day to see the child, dragging his shrunken little limbs, trying to reach the butterflies that danced in the sunshine, month by month to watch his baby body grow into rosy loveliness—and helplessness.

Every evening at vespers, every morning at matins, did she pray, unceasingly, yet with an inner sense of futility, for the sin of too much loving to be forgiven her; for the punishment of too much love to be lifted from the innocent life of her child.

In the confessional she poured out her sin—that she had loved too much. But the curé said, very gently, "That was no sin, my daughter. It was a great virtue."

"Then," she did not realize the passionate resentment in her voice, "why is my child punished for a sin which he did not commit—no, which you tell me even *I* did not commit?" The curé sighed, and twisted his fingers a little. It was hard to always tell her that it was God's will, and yet his cloth, his religion, demanded it.

"My daughter," he hesitated, "dark and strange are the ways of the good God. Perhaps it is a test of your

devotion and faith, my child. Perhaps He is waiting to
work a miracle—"

The girl's eyes widened. "Père Touraine," she
gasped, "do you really, then, believe in miracles?"

"Oh, certainly," he answered readily, this time surer
of his ground. "This history of Holy Church is filled
with them."

"Ah—history," she sighed dejectedly, "history is so
far off—it is gone."

The summer passed, and the autumn. The leaves
were blown from the shivering trees, the air was filled
with the cold tang of approaching winter. The first
snow came, and the children played in it joyously,
shouting inarticulately and rolling it into balls.
Jeanette watched from the windows of the inn, watched
with heavy, dark eyes, that were always widely
stretched as if with unshed tears.

"*My* child," she whispered to herself, "will never
play like that—never, never." Then one snowy day in
December, at the time when the children were beginning to talk excitely of what Saint Nicholas would
leave in their wooden shoes, a stranger came to the
inn—a curious, silent man, with deep-set, fanatical
eyes, and an agitated way of moving his hands when
he spoke. He wore the smock and sheep-skin coat of
a peasant. Jeanette served him, as she served all pa-
trons of the inn, silently, apathetically, with eyes
that never wavered from their stedfast look of misery.
But when her baby cried, wrapped in swathings of
blankets, the man looked up and saw her face, and put
out his hand to detain her as she turned away.

"The little one, Madame, he is yours?"

"Yes, M'sieu," she said without moving.

"Is there anything—forgive me if I intrude myself

too much—is there anything wrong with the child? I saw your face just now, when he cried, and I thought—"

She bent her head slightly.

"He was born a cripple, M'sieu. His little limbs are paralyzed."

The man's eyes blazed up suddenly like a torch flame in a dark vault. He caught her wrist, half drew her down to him.

"Listen, little one! Attend me! You will be thankful for having listened to my words. Listen, and believe me. There is a little town near Pierrefitte where miracles are performed in the church, every Eve of Noël, just by touching the crib of the little Jesus that is outside the altar railing." The doors of her heart seemed suddenly to open, to receive a great flood of light and warmth.

"M'sieu," she gasped, clutching at his arm, "you do not mock me? Miracles are really performed in that way?" The man's eyes gleamed in their deep-set sockets.

"My child, you see before you one who was cured, whose limbs dragged and were useless, even as are the limbs of your little one. And I was healed by touching the manger of the little Jesus, as many others have been healed, and as all will be healed who have the faith to take advantage of the precious moments of divine manifestation."

Careless of the frowning glances of Madame Luconne, Jeanette sank down before the stranger, fumbling with her apron. A momentary weakness had sapped her of strength. She could only stare at the man and whisper, with dry, tense lips, "Tell me more, M'sieu, tell me everything about it. I will not lack the faith, if only I know what must be done."

The man bent above her, and lowered his voice. His strange, restless hands moved continually.

"Do you know the village of Viendoncourt?"

"No, M'sieu, but I can find it."

"Almost eighty kilometers from here it lies. The nearest railroad is Pierrefitte. The village of Viendoncourt lies three miles along the road from there, or a mile or two across the fields."

"Yes, yes, M'sieu, I can find it. But what of the church, the manger, what of the miracles of the Eve of Noël?"

"Come closer, little one, this message is holy. There is a tradition that angels, bearing the little Jesus to his mother for birth, passed close above the spot. And it must be true, it *is* true! For every Noël's Eve, just as the chalice is being raised in the midnight mass, *there comes a great rushing of wings,* and a multitude of unseen singers crying, 'Kyrie Elieson, Kyrie Elieson!' *That* is the moment, little one. The air is filled with the rustling of angels' wings, the sweeping of their garments, the ecstasy of their presence. At that moment, he who would be healed has but to touch the crib by the altar rail, and he shall be made whole."

"But—but—" she stammered, "my baby cannot pray."

"No, but you, his mother, can. And your voice in petition will reach the angels as they pass over. Behold me, little one! I was cured thus. Look at my limbs. They are strong and sturdy. They were lame, useless, like the baby's there."

He arose abruptly, stared out at the snowy twilight, and fumbled for his cap.

"Yes, like the baby's there," he mumbled, flung

down a coin on the table, and passed out into the snow and the darkness.

Jeanette sat staring after him as in a dream. Vaguely she heard her baby crying, and the sharp voice of Madame Luconne.

"Get up, you lazy bones! The brat is crying and there are dirty dishes upon the table. Do I pay you for idle chatter with strange men? Get up, you good-for-nothing!"

Still as one in a trance, Jeanette pulled herself up to her feet. Then she turned her pale, transfigured face upon her mistress. "Madame," she said jerkily, "that man, just now, he told me a wonderful thing. There are miracles still. There is a little church where I must go, on Noël's Eve, carrying my baby to be healed—" Madame Luconne laughed shortly.

"Miracles, my girl, are for priests and saints. You are neither. Clear off the dishes, and stop that baby's crying." But Jeanette stood her ground, her eyes burning with a fixed, intense light.

"Madame, he spoke the truth. I feel it here in my heart. And I must reach that place by Noël's Eve." She started suddenly. "Why, that is only five days away. May I have my wages, Madame Luconne, so that I may leave by to-morrow's train?"

"Your wages," said the other woman deliberately, "are not due for this month until after Noël. If I give them to you now you will be off on this wild-goose chase, and I will be out a servant—for the holidays, too. No, Jeanette, don't be a fool. Your baby is what God intended him to be, a hopeless cripple."

A great cry surged up from the heart and lips of the girl. A hot flush burned in her blanched cheeks. She seemed suddenly to increase in stature and dignity.

"No," she cried, "no! It has been, as Père Touraine said, a test of patience, of waiting, and of faith. The stranger was a messenger of the good God, to tell me that a miracle was about to make my little one whole. I will go, I *will* go, do you hear? If not by train, then I will walk. I shall carry my baby in my arms, and no harm will come to us! The good God and His angels will protect us!" She caught up her baby from the hearth, wrapped him closely with the blankets on which he had been lying. Then, snatching her thin, ragged shawl from behind the door, flung it about her head and shoulders.

"Stop, you little idiot," cried Madame Luconne sharply. But the door of the inn opened, and slammed shut, blowing in a flurry of snow; shutting out the girl Jeanette with her burden of helplessness—and faith.

All the long night the girl walked along the snowy road that led north towards Viendoncourt. She had to rest many times, for her arms were stiff with the unaccustomed weight, and her feet became numb with the cold. But the snow had ceased to fall. The moon came out from behind white, billowy clouds, and all the world a-shimmer with silver light. There was no wind, and the cold had lessened. So the girl, who had stopped under the protecting shadow of a wayside shrine, nursed her baby and smiled with the warm, contented joy as the little lips nuzzled against her breast. Then she went on, the only living thing upon the road of silver and moonlight, and the baby slept, with its downy head snuggled into the warm wrapping of the blanket.

When the first grayness of dawn was upon the sleeping world, the girl realized suddenly that she was very tired. She had no way of knowing how many kilometers she had come, for her knowledge of the world was bounded by the village of Beaucoeur, where she had lived all her life. When she saw a farm house with smoke creeping up into the grayness of the sky, she knocked at the door, and astonished the peasant and his wife, who were just ready to commence the early morning chores.

"Might I ask for a little milk?" she faltered. "I have come a long way—"

The heat of the room swept toward her in an overwhelming wave, making her very drowsy. She swayed as she stood in the doorway, and the two peasants staring at her became unreal and wrapped in a hazy mist.

"A very—long—way—" she repeated, and sank down gently, with her eyes drooping shut. When she awoke, it was with a delicious feeling of warmth and lassitude. There were little homely noises about her, the cluck of chickens, the soft snapping of a fire, the distant crowing of a rooster, the scraping of a chair on the floor. Then, as realization came back to her, she sat up sharply, pushing back the quilt that had been laid over her. There was an ache in her arms that made her wince with pain when she moved them. The peasant woman was regarding her kindly and with frank curiosity.

"Well," she said heartily, "you have slept long and soundly. Tired indeed you were, little one."

"My baby—" said the girl faintly, still dazed with sleep.

"Oh, the little chick is safe enough, lying over there in the sunshine trying to play with his toes. His legs— forgive me— are they not—"

The girl burst into sudden tears.

"Oh, yes, Madame—they are paralyzed. And I could sleep! I could forget the needs of my little one! Tell me, I beg of you, how far have I come from Beaucoeur?"

"Beaucoeur? Oh, perhaps seven or eight kilometers. You walked all the way last night?"

The peasant woman's tone became a little suspicious. "Yes, yes—but oh, that is not far enough. I have so far to go, so very far—and I could sleep!" She went to her baby, whose mouth was puckered into intent concentration. He was trying his best to reach his toes, to bring up the little shrunken limbs so that he could try to taste of the limp white foot. An empty nursing bottle lay beside him.

"Oh, Madame," the girl said with tears still in her eyes, "I thank you for your goodness. I am trying to reach Viendoncourt by Noël's Eve, where a miracle will make my baby well. I thought my faith and courage would be stronger than to let myself sleep as I did."

The peasant woman shook her head dubiously. "Miracles?" she repeated. "I am afraid—Well, well, at any rate, refresh yourself with milk and bread. If you must go so far, you must not neglect the needs of your body."

Jeanette ate and drank ravenously, hastily. The sun, well past the high point of noon, was a constant reproach to her. The peasant woman busied herself with sewing the blankets into a kind of pouch, so that the baby could be carried upon the girl's back. Then she brought out a quantity of unspun wool and put it in the bag.

"This will make the journey more comfortable for you,—and for him," she said practically.

Then she wrapped a piece of black bread in a paper and gave it to the girl.

"May the good God bless you for your kindness!" said Jeanette, gratefully. "As soon as I can spare the prayers from my baby's needs, I will remember you every night."

"Good luck to you—and the miracle!" responded the peasant woman, watching her from the doorway.

Now upon the third day, when she was so utterly weary of mind and body that she felt nothing, only a numb and constant aching in her limbs and shoulders, she realized that a hearty voice was hailing her, and that a team of oxen had stopped beside her. A young man, with ruddy face and smiling blue eyes, walked beside them with a long goad pole in his hand.

"A good day to you, Mam'selle," he greeted her. "You look tired. You may ride upon my wagon, if you like." She turned her pale, set face upon him, and he was conscious, with a shock of surprize, that she stared through him, as if he had been a window.

"Thank you," she said in a dull, heavy voice, "I am a little tired. I will be glad to ride—if you are going towards Viendoncourt."

"Viendoncourt?" He puckered his lips in a whistle. "You are going as far as that, Mam'selle—Madame?" He had just realized that the bundle on her back which made her droop forward so tiredly was a baby.

"Yes, I must be there by Noël's Eve. I *must* be there." He helped her up on the rough wagon, with its load of hay. He packed it closely around her so that she should not be cold.

"Well," he said, touching the oxen with his goad, and walking beside the wagon, "you are still a long way from Viendoncourt—almost thirty kilometers. I am not going that far myself. I turn off at Lienne. You must be there by the Eve of Noël, you say?"

"Yes, M'sieur," she answered dully, yet with unshakable finality, "I must be there."

He walked beside her in silence, and the girl was silent too. Presently her feet began to ache terribly, and she lowered the sleeping baby for a moment to rub them. The leaning down made her weak with dizziness. She toppled forward in the hay.

Quickly the young man sprang up beside her, lifted her up and laid her gently back in the hay. But she struggled up to a sitting posture.

"No—no, M'sieu," she gasped, "I dare not lie down. I must not sleep—I have so far to go!"

Then for the first time he realized the tragic intensity of her dark eyes, the blue circles under them, and the wan, pinched cheeks. He took the baby very quietly from her arms, and she began to cry jerkily, in spite of her efforts at self control, as her tensed muscles relaxed and ached.

"There, there," he said soothingly, as if she had been a child, "you are tired—and hungry, too, without a doubt. Here!" He opened a leather sack and took out bread, cold cabbage and cheese. She ate slowly, despite the terrible hunger that was consuming her. And he watched her with distress in his honest blue eyes. Presently she sighed, and sat back, and smiled wanly at him. He smiled too, with a great breath of relief.

"There now, you feel better, I wager!" he cried, much pleased that his efforts at caring for her had been so successful.

"You are—" he hesitated, unwilling to appear too

curious, "you are going to visit relatives—or perhaps to join your—husband?"

"I have no husband," she replied simply.

"Oh," he stammered, making pretense of striking at the oxen.

"No, M'sieu, I go to the church at Viendoncourt, where at midnight on Noël's Eve, a miracle will be performed that will make my baby well. See, M'sieu—this is my reason for the journey."

She unfolded the blankets for the merest instant, disclosing the white, shrunken limbs. She picked one up, tenderly, and it fell from her fingers, lifeless, inanimate. Then she wrapped the blankets once more about the sleeping child.

Through the long, sunlit winter day the girl rode in the wagon, and the young man walked or sat for a few moments beside her, dangling his legs, and smoking a pipe. When noon time came he insisted on a halt at a village inn, and made her join him in a hot and hearty meal. Then they went on, and already there was a little color in the girl's pale cheeks, and once or twice she smiled wanly at his descriptions of people he knew and of happenings at the fair. He liked to see her, riding there in the hay, with the baby at her feet, and he sighed a little when he thought of how soon she would be gone, and that he would not see her again.

At last they approached Lienne, where the roads forked. He was walking moodily by the wagon, striking the ground with the ox goad. Presently he looked up at the girl, his pleasant face flushed and glowing.

"You will pardon me if I seem too bold," he said with some difficulty, "but nothing is ever gained by letting a golden moment slip by. Yonder is where the road divides, and I must go on to Crué because I

have promised this hay to my cousin there. Now—
now," he took a long breath and looked at her boldly,
"now must you go to Viendoncourt? Look you,
Madame, I am unmarried. I have a little farm that
makes me a good living. I can afford a servant—yes,
easily, for I am a hard worker. I have not cared much
for women, of this I assure you, for all the girls I
have known seem very silly and giggling. Would you
not—would you not consider going on with me to Crué,
and standing up with me in the church at the morning
mass on Noël? I have faults, yes, certainly. But I
have no bad temper—and I am fond of children."

She stared at him with wide, startled eyes.

"Why—why, M'sieu," she faltered, "that is impossible. I have told you about the little one—"

"Yes, yes, I know," he said eagerly, "but come now,
miracles do not really happen nowadays. And many
children are cripples, yet they live well and happily.
I would make the little fellow a swinging chair, so that
he could play in the sunshine all day. Believe me,
Madame, I would be good to him—and you."

"I am sure of that," she said in a low tone, "but—"

For the moment he misunderstood her. "If you
are thinking of the baby's having no father, do not let
that trouble you. These things happen. It does not
matter."

A hot flush suffused her pale face.

"M'sieu," she said with dignity, "my *husband* is
dead."

"Oh," he said, biting his lips, "I beg your forgiveness,
truly I do."

"It does not matter," she said gently. "In any case,
I must go on. I must reach Viendoncourt by the Eve

of Noël. I cannot think of anything else—I assure you I cannot, M'sieu."

"Well, well then," he persisted, "what will you do after you have accomplished your purpose in Viendoncourt?"

"I do not know," she said dully, "I have no plans."

"You will stay a little while in that town—just a little while?" he begged. "Look you, I will be in Crué by tomorrow night at the latest. I can leave my team there and come by train to Pierrefitte and walk over to Viendoncourt. I can be there early on Noël. Only say that I will find you there, and that we can talk further."

For the first time she consciously saw his face. And it came to her with a shock that there was something about him which reminded her of Pierre—perhaps the blueness of his eyes, or the way he was always laughing.

But she shook her head gently. "M'sieu, you are very good. But I can promise nothing. All my mind, all my heart, is set stedfastly on the single purpose of making my baby well. I should be unworthy of God's great love and His willingness to work a miracle for my little one if I gave one thought to my own comfort or future." He smiled at her, and it did not seem as if he took her words for a refusal.

"I like that in you, too, Madame. Well, you must go on, I can see that. And may God be good to you and give you your heart's desire. But remember, I too now have a heart's desire. I shall be in Viendoncourt on Noël, and shall seek you at the church, or at the curé's home." They had come to the forking of the road. He regretfully helped her to alight and put the baby in her arms.

"Good-by," he shouted back at her, "remember, I will be there on Noël morning!"

She stood looking after him for a moment, and a little sigh escaped her lips. Her back already felt the strain of its burden. It had been nice to ride in the hay, with the baby playing at her feet. But after an instant's pause she turned, set her face northward, and went forward on her long journey.

Far into the night she walked without stopping, except for the briefest moments. The coldness became bitter and well nigh unendurable. She began to stamp her feet as she walked, and to swing her arms. But gradually the dreadful need of sleep came upon her, insidious, overpowering. She walked with sagging, uncertain steps, forced on only by the inner strength of her resolution. Suddenly there came an end, an involuntary slumping of her body. She sank down listly in the snow. The baby cried sharply, and she stirred drowsily.

"I must not, must not sleep!" she heard herself saying. She struggled to her feet, and saw through the dim darkness a stable ahead of her. She staggered to the door, thrust it open, and fell exhausted upon the hay.

Next morning she wrapped the baby warmly in the blankets, swung it again upon her back. She pushed the stable door open, and shivered as the icy coldness swept in upon her.

"And yet," she said, lifting her face to the dull sky, "tomorrow will be the Eve of Noël. I have come this far by the grace of the good God. Surely strength will be given me to come safely to the church of the great miracle."

It was the Eve of Noël. The lights were lit in every window of Pierrefitte. There was the sound of laughter and of music.

In the little church the lights of many candles gleamed, and in front of the altar was an amazingly realistic stable, with its manger, and kneeling oxen, its shepherds and its wise men, and last but not least, the mother and Child.

There were many people in the street, and many calls of "Joyous Noël, neighbor!" The snow was fluttering down in soft, caressing flakes. At the end of a narrow street a band of children were singing carols. Their high treble voices broke into laughter as a door opened, and a shower of cakes and candies was thrown out at them. Softly, clearly, came the tolling of the church bell, ringing for the midnight mass.

The curé's sister, who shared with him the little stone house beside the church, had just put on her bonnet and cape. There came a knock at the door, a curious, pounding knock, as if the person outside was beating on the door with clinched fists.

She smiled, thinking it the prank of boys, or perhaps some hearty peasant stopping to leave an offering of poultry for the curé. Still smiling, she opened the door wide, and caught her breath with the unexpectedness of what she saw—a girl, snow-covered, hollow-eyed, with lips that were blue and pinched, stood there, trembling, clasping a bundle in her arms.

"Is this—the curé's house?" she said with difficulty.

"Yes, yes," answered the curé's sister, regaining her faculties with practical swiftness. "Come in, and God be with you." She pushed forward a chair, but the girl still stood in the doorway, swaying.

"No, Madame," she said in the same flat, barely audi-

ble voice, "I cannot sit down—I dare not. There is
very little strength left in me, and I must save it—
This is Viendoncourt, is it not?"

"No," said the curé's sister briskly, "this is Pierrefitte. Viendoncourt lies three miles along the road, or
one may cut across the fields, a mile and a little over."

She was startled by the wrenching cry of the girl
before her.

"*Not* Viendoncourt! Oh, Madame—I thought I had
reached the end of my journey. I am afraid I cannot
go on—"

The curé's sister pushed the girl into a chair.

"Well, well, is it so important, my child? You are
tired, and there is a warm bed that will give you shelter
for tonight."

"Ah, *so* important!" cried the girl, who had heard
only the first words. "I must be in the church at Viendoncourt at the midnight mass when the chalice is
lifted. I must lay my baby in the manger so that he
may become cured of his sickness!"

The curé's sister stared at the swaying, ragged figure.
"You have a baby there? And it is sick?"

"Yes, Madam, look!" The girl drew back the
blankets and showed the tiny body, with its shrunken,
paste-white limbs.

The curé's sister exclaimed with pity.

"The poor little one! But why do you take him
to the church at Viendoncourt? I do not understand."

"For the miracle, Madam, the miracle!"

"The miracle?" repeated the woman in a puzzled
tone. "What miracle do you expect, my child?"

"Oh, Madame, surely you have heard of it, since the
town is so near! At midnight, when the chalice is
lifted in the mass, there comes a great rushing of wings,,

and unseen voices chanting 'Kyrie Elieson, Kyrie Elieson!' and at that moment if one but touches the manger of the little Jesus outside the altar rail, all sickness is cured. Surely you have known of miracles being thus effected?"

The curé's sister was looking at the girl with a strange expression of dismay and uncertainty. A phrase in the girl's impassioned recital had caught her ear, and echoed now in her mind.

"Oh, my poor child," she exclaimed at last, "you must not go. You must wait until my brother, the curé, comes back from midnight mass. He will tell you—"

But the girl had risen wildly to her feet.

"The midnight mass!" she cried sharply. "It has begun."

As if in answer, came the distant tinkle of the sacristy bell.

The girl rushed to the door, flung it open, and staggered outside. "Which way, which way, for the love of God?"

The curé's sister sought to stop her, but it was like stopping the wind.

"Child, child!" she called, but the girl was out upon the street.

"Which way, Madame—the field you spoke of?"

Helplessly the curé's sister pointed. She called out again, but the girl had disappeared, stumbling through the snow, with the baby clasped tight against her breast. The curé's sister shut the door and stood frowning.

"My brother should know of this," she murmured to herself.

Where before, the girl had plodded heavily, almost

numb from lack of sleep and rest, now she ran stumbling and sobbing, plunging off across the field that spread out, broad and white as a funeral sheet, toward the distant town of Viendoncourt, where the church steeple and the roofs were black against the sky. The snow had ceased to fall, but the girl did not know. A raging blizzard could not have stopped her or turned her aside. Her running feet crunched on the brittle surface of the field, but now and then there would come a soft spot through which she fell, almost up to her knees.

An insane recklessness had seized upon her now, a defiant disregard for obstacles; for the cold, for the racking breath that cut her lungs as with a knife, for the crying of the jostled baby.

"There, there, my little one," she said through clenched teeth, "if I hurt you, forgive me. There is no time now to be gentle. We must reach the church in time—we must reach there before the chalice is raised—"

She ran on and on. Her breath came in whistled snatches. There was a red mist before her eyes. No matter—no matter—The baby cried shrilly, twisting its imprisoned body as best it could. No matter—no matter—with glazed eyes, with mouth half open, with sagging, desperate feet, she ran on—on! Now the houses loomed more plainly against the sky. Viendoncourt—at last!

Soon the houses rose up all round her as if by magic. She was swaying like a drunken woman, reeling from side to side. She could not see. There were shadows, shadows everywhere—houses—where was the church? There were lights in windows—but how to reach them. She staggered towards the nearest one. She pitched

forward headlong on the step of some building. She
lay there for a moment, stunned. But the snow was
soft and had broken her fall. She beat the snow out
of her all but blinded eyes.

"Oh God, oh God," she sobbed out, "do not let me
fail now—show me the way—give me a sign—"

And then—from within the place—there came *a
great rushing of wings!*

The girl heard, and suddenly the blood went thrill-
ing throughout her body. As in a trance she rose
from the snowy step. From far away, unseen voices
were singing, swelling out in a great chant of triumph,
"Keyrie, Keyrie, Kristi elieson!"

Her eyes were shining as if with inner fire. She held
forth the babe on her outstretched hands as a priest
lifts up an offering to the Most High.

"God is good!" she whispered in ecstasy, and pushed
open the door.

"And you let her go out on a fool's chase like that?"
the curé stormed at his sister. "You did not tell her?"

"How could I?" she defended herself. "I thought
it best for you to tell her. Besides, she rushed away
before I could say a word."

"Damnation!" swore the curé. "Oh, yes, I know I
will have to confess it," he snapped at his sister's
shocked face, "but it is really too much. That madman with his tales of miracles—see what harm he
may have done! Ever since he was studying for the
priesthood, and the church caved in upon him, he has
become obsessed with rustling of wings, and sickness
miraculously cured. Harmless they call him, and let
him roam at will. But this is a case which proves how
wrong the authorities are. His mania takes the form

of believing himself cured of the exact thing which he sees at the time—fever, the pox, lameness, and now, paralysis! Have I not had my troubles telling poor, misguided souls that his tales are nothing but a madman's dream? And this poor girl! Good God, she may have perished in the snow!"

Without further words he jammed on his broad-brimmed hat and his thickest cape, and lighting a lantern, set out across the snowy fields.

When the curé reached the village of Viendoncourt, breathless and panting from his forced pace through the snow, the mass was long since over, the church was emptied, the windows were dark. He searched the recesses of the small church carefully. He found no one.

As he came out, pausing, hesitant, not knowing where to look, a peasant in sheepskin coat and fur cap came stumbling awkwardly toward him.

"M'sieu, le curé," he gasped out, "would it please your holiness to come with me? Perhaps I am drunk, or dreaming—"

He turned about the corner of the church, to where a stone building loomed against the holy edifice, the two standing back to back. He ran around to the front, and hesitated upon the step. "In—in—there!" He whispered, pointing at the door. The priest pushed open the heavy door, and stood with upraised lantern.

Perhaps he too was dreaming, but it seemed to him that a great radiance flooded the stable—surely a greater radiance than the lantern hanging over the manger, or the one held in his hand, could give; a great, golden light that glowed softly and warmly, just above the manger, where, upon a bed of fragrant hay, a little baby lay gurgling and laughing up at the light, and stretching out his hands, catching at play with the tiny feet, which were kicking into the air, pounding against the blankets, burrowing into the hay.

At the foot of the manger sat a woman—a girl. Her eyes were closed, and she slept deeply, with a smile like the glory of heaven upon her tired, contented lips. The golden light seemed to surround her in an aura of golden fire. And near her the cattle drowsed, munching contentedly at the hay.

"M'sieu, le curé," whispered the peasant to the transfixed priest, "is it, can it be the Mother and Child who have honored my humble stable on this night of Noël? See your holiness, I left a lantern burning there above the manger, because of a sickly calf which I wished to look at after mass, and when I came back, the pigeons were flying about, aroused by the light—I heard the rushing of their wings—and when I came in—these two were here! Is it, *is it* a miracle, father?"

The voice of the priest was hoarse and trembling. "A miracle, indeed, my son, a blessed miracle of faith!"

The light had died away. Only the dimness of the lanterns pierced the fragrant gloom. The curé went softly towards the sleeping woman and the laughing baby who was sucking at his rosy, wriggling toes.

"Blessed are the pure in heart," he whispered, "for they shall see God!"

Then he stood still, startled, thrilled to the heart by a distant sound,—*a great rushing of wings.*

He held the lantern high. No pigeons were flying. They slept quietly upon the rafters of the stable.

MR. ONION

By Dana Burnet

It was when she went to turn out the light back of the sofa that Marian discovered Mr. Onion perched on top of the bookshelves. Dressed in his perennial clown's costume, and holding in his hands the ladder that was an integral part of his character, he stood patiently grinning down at her. His grin was ludicrous. It was also faintly pathetic, as every true clown's grin should be.

Marian thought: Jackie must have climbed up on the sofa last night before he went to bed and put Mr. Onion on top of the bookshelves. . . . Funny that I never noticed him there. . . . But I was so busy with things . . . people. . . . Good Lord! What a party! They must have had a good time. . . . They stayed till daylight. . . . But our crowd always has a good time. . . .

"I'll take Mr. Onion back to the nursery; Jackie adores him. . . . He cares more for that clown than for all his other toys put together. . . ."

But when she reached for the little wooden figure a weakness seized her. She began to laugh hysterically. She was so very tired and Mr. Onion was so very absurd. So unalterably absurd. . . . And so pathetic. . . . It was the way his painted mouth turned up at the corners. . . .

She sank down on the sofa, shaking with uncontrollable laughter. John came stumbling in from their bedroom. His coat was off, and his tie dangled like a wilted purple flag from his loosened collar.

" 'Matter, old girl?"

"Look! F-funny. . . ."

"Oh, Mr. Onion?"

"Y-e-e-s!"

"But what's funny? Where's the joke?"

"I—don't—know. I think it's his grin. . . . No, it's the l-ladder," gasped Marian helplessly. "Why must he always carry a ladder? It's so p-pointless."

"Everything's pointless at five o'clock in the morning," grumbled John, yawning. "Come to bed, Marian. You're worn out. So am I. The damned party lasted too long," he added, with sudden irritability.

"To think of Mr. Onion's standing up there all night watching us!" said Marian, sighing. "I wonder what he thought of us?"

"Sick of parties," said John. "Come to bed—"

But somehow they didn't go to bed just then. The great rush of light across the sea and up the hill and through the windows of their cottage may have struck them all at once as something too precious to be wasted. Or possibly they were still a trifle dizzy from the effect of their own hospitality and wanted to cool their heads in the fresh morning air; or possibly they were just too exhausted to do anything very definite. . . .

They drifted out-of-doors and sat down on the rustic bench that stood at the edge of the hill, facing the sea. . . . Marian, in her crumpled evening dress, with her black hair curling flatly about her pretty, tired face, with something rather strange and crumpled in her eyes, was a mildly fascinating figure to John, her husband. They had been married six years, he reflected remotely. Nice to know that Marian could still turn into a woman he never had seen before.

But was there, perhaps, a chance, a slight chance, that some day she might turn into a complete—and permanent—stranger? He had watched her last night dancing with Tom Nevinson. Nevinson was keen on Marian. He had fallen for her in the frankly casual way that men now fell for other men's wives. It was a case according to the modern code. Also according to the modern code John Thurston was forbidden the old-fashioned emotion of jealousy. . . . Besides, wasn't he himself more or less engaged in making love to Sally Nevinson, Tom's pert, blond wife? Nevertheless, he recalled, if not with jealousy, at least with amazement, the difference in Marian when she danced or joked or flirted with Tom. For of course she did flirt. All nice women flirted nowadays. . . . Well, what of it? They always had. . . . Only not so openly.

"I wonder what Mr. Onion *does* think of us?"

"What's on your mind, sweetheart?"

But she didn't answer directly, and his own mind floated off and away like a bit of cloud—like that fleecy cloud being driven into the sunrise by the light western breeze. It would be a fine, fair day, said his high-sailing mind. . . .

He wanted vaguely to ask Marian a question—something that would involve and bring to an issue all the unasked and unanswered questions between them. But the only thing he could think of was: Where did Mr. Onion come from?

He couldn't remember, at the moment, who had given
Jackie that ridiculous clown. His lapse of memory
annoyed him. It invested Mr. Onion with a certain
mystery; with a certain importance.

Oh, nonsense! Why not ask Marian? Of course
she would know. She could recite offhand the origin
and history of any of Jackie's toys. But he wouldn't
ask her. He wouldn't be so silly. As tho there
could be any mystery about a child's plaything!

"By the way, Marian, whoever gave Jackie that
darned clown?"

"I don't know," answered his wife absently.

"What? You must know!"

"Well, I don't. We were never able to find out.
. . . Don't you remember? He just turned up
that Christmas, and we never knew who sent him. We
never found the card. I made quite an effort, too—
asked everyone I could think of—because Jackie
adored him so. But I never found out. . . ."

"Uh-huh," said John.

"It was Jackie who named him," added Marian,
with a sleepy, reminiscent smile. . . . She could
hear, by some mental process that was more than
memory, little Jackie's grave, childish voice murmuring in her ears, drumming at her heart. . . . "The
clown's name is Mr. Onion. He has a funny name
because clowns are funny people. And he has a ladder
because he likes it. He can do tricks on it if he wants
to. But he'd rather just carry it. It makes him feel
like he was going to climb something."

Marian smiled, thinking of Jackie still asleep in his
safe, white bed, in the wing of the cottage which they
had built five years ago when he was born. Safe bed,

safe house, safe beautiful country. . . . The Maine shore in August. . . . No place on earth more perfect for a child!

All safe! Yet, curiously, deep down in her tired body, in her brooding mind, she was aware of a blankness, a shadow that was almost fear. Life, in its essence, was so fragile. . . . And there was so much of it that was mere doubt and dream and nebulous, swiftly changing chemical reaction. . . .

"We have no God," she said abruptly but very simply, as tho uttering a familiar and common-place thought.

John stirred beside her. He uncrossed and stretched his long flannel-clad legs. "And what," he asked, "would we be doing with a God if we had one?"

"Oh, I don't know. Pray to Him. . . . Depend on Him. . . . Have Him in for tea—and conversation."

"You've been looking at the sun. It's made you religious," he said.

"The sun's too impersonal," replied Marian. "Sometimes when you want it most it goes under a cloud. . . . I'd rather like a God," she continued murmurously, "who would always be on hand in case of—of emergency."

John twisted about, with an effort, to look at her. "Are you serious, old girl?"

"Serious? Yes, I think so."

"How come? What's the big idea? We've got along all right so far without any particular household deity."

"Have we?" breathed Marian.

"Well, haven't we?" he countered.

"I don't know," she said again slowly. "I wonder—

I can't help wondering whether we, whether people like us—our generation—are as successful at living as we like to think we are. We pretend to a good deal of—advancement. Progress. . . . But I'm not so sure. We've dragged out a lot of the old bugaboos and made faces at them. We've learned to admit that we have bodies, and we've organized a parade of the senses—with Papa Freud as drum major. We've abolished vice by the simple process of making a virtue of it. And maybe these things help. They're a kind of oil—banana oil—that we keep pouring out to smooth over the surface! But there's something volcanic at the center. I feel it—so often! A kind of restlessness, an uncertainty, as tho we were living over a storm that might break at any moment—"

"Don't," said John placidly. "What's the use?"

"You feel it too!"

"Well—yes—in a way. Who doesn't? But—no good expecting things to happen. Besides, what can happen to us? I mean, barring some accident."

"That's just it. Accidents do happen. Oh, why not admit that it's all accident? And—the trouble with us is that we've never been *through* anything. We don't know our own strength or our own weakness—"

"Oh, well," interrupted John, "we've got—anyway—a philosophy. A kind of philosophy. At least I have." He glanced at her rather defiantly, but she was staring at the golden east, at the infinite cobalt sea. "I believe in myself, in my own vitality—"

"Yes, dear, I know." This was the modern credo. She had heard it so many times before.

"Vitality's the only virtue. Be a good animal! Take Jackie, for instance. People are always harping on what a healthy kid he is—as tho that were some sort of accident. It makes me sore! Why shouldn't he be healthy?" demanded Jackie's father. "You and I are healthy, decent people. He's our child. There's a kind of reason in it, a kind of logic."

"But life so frequently isn't logical," objected Marian in a voice as distant as her gaze. "There's so often a gap, a vacancy, a lost link in the chain—"

"I don't feel that. I have my work, you know." He was a trifle stiff with fatigue.

"Does it satisfy you? Does your painting really satisfy you?"

"If it didn't, why would I go on with it?"

"Why not? One has to do something. . . . I've suspected, at times, that it was simply a slave to your conscience, an excuse for loafing," she said with a frankness born, perhaps, of sheer physical exhaustion.

"I see," grunted John. Then he laughed shortly. "Hell! as long as we're telling our real names this morning, I'd like to know—if you don't mind—just how much that bird Nevinson means in your young life?"

"Tom?" Her voice was a languid note in the increasing breeze. "Does Tom strike you as being—important?"

"Not as a person, perhaps. But as a symptom—"

"Yes, I grant you that. Tom may be a symptom. . . . Of what, I wonder? Because I really don't know. I'm not a promiscuous sort of woman, am I? Do you think I am?"

"I hope not," answered her husband.

"Why do I bother with Tom at all? Why do you
bother with Sally?"

"Oh, Sally. . . ." mumbled John.

"You kissed her last night. I saw you. . . .
When you were dancing on the porch. Tom hasn't
kissed me—yet. Not really. But he will. It's coming
to that. I suppose I'm a fool to tell you this, but
I do so want to know why. . . . Because we—
you and I—actually care a lot about each other, don't
we, John dear?"

"Why, sure, a lot! A whole lot! Sure, we do."
He was awkward and boyish in his desire to be
emphatic. He put his hand on her arm. "Let's chuck
it," he said. "Let's not play this silly game any more.
You're right about my work. It *is* an excuse. But
I was thinking. . . . if I could get away, go
somewhere . . . to Paris, maybe. We've got
money enough to do what we please. Let's pull up
stakes and beat it—"

She shook briefly her small, dark head.

"Paris is only another place. 'The fault, dear
Brutus' . . ." The rest of the quotation was lost
in the wind. "You'd find the same silly game in Paris,
or wherever you decided to go. . . . Only it isn't
silly. It's desperately serious. . . . The trouble
is at the center. . . . What we lack is a faith—
some faith—in something—beyond ourselves." Her
speech was broken into staccato bits, and the spaces
were filled by the rustling of leaves, by the muffled
drumbeat of the surf on the beach a quarter of a mile
away. "That's why we go looking into other people.
. . . Always prying into other people, hoping,
hoping to find the prophet of some true God. . . ."

"You'll find no prophet in Tom Nevinson," growled John.

"Perhaps not. But I'll go on looking just the same. I must look! Don't you see? I can't afford not to. I might be cheated out of some miracle. If only I could find that miracle in you," she said quietly, and turned toward him her strange, searching, weary eyes.

He took her in his arms and kissed her.

"No," he said. "I won't pose. I won't play prophet or promise miracles ven to make you happy. I'm not up to a hair shirt and a diet of locusts. If you can't be satisfied with a plain man who—oh, hell!" he broke off sharply. "Let's quit this. We're getting in too deep. It's just because we're so darned tired. What are we sitting out here for, anyway? Let's go in—have some breakfast—go to bed."

Miss Mosby, little Jackie's nurse, appeared in her chaste white as they sat dispiritedly at breakfast on the screened dining porch.

"Jackie has a little cold this morning," said Miss Mosby.

"Don't let him go into the ocean, then," cautioned Marian.

"Very well, Mrs. Thurston."

"How much of a cold?" asked John, stifling a yawn.

"His nose is running," announced Miss Mosby, smoothing her prophylactic apron.

"Maybe he oughtn't to go to the beach at all," worried Marian.

"Oh, nonsense!" said her husband. "Beautiful, warm day like this. Do him good to be down there in the sunshine. . . . I'll have a look at him."

He got up and went into Jackie's room.

"Hello, Big Boy! Hear you got the snuffles?"

"But not a cold," quickly replied Jackie, sitting up in bed.

"Well, I don't know. How do you feel?"

"Fine, Daddy! I don't feel sick at all. I guess I can go to the beach all right," added Jackie, and squirmed uneasily as his father seemed to deliberate. "I guess it would do me a lot of good to go to the beach, all right!"

"Beautiful day," thought John. What could happen to a healthy kid on a day like this? Well, for the love of Pete, what did he *think* was going to happen? "My nerves are shot," he decided: "staying up all night, drinking. . . . I'm jumpy. And, then, that queer talk with Marian! What was it she'd said about life being so uncertain, so—fragile—?

"Why, sure," he decided finally. "The beach—sure! Only, I wouldn't go in bathing to-day, if I were you, Big Boy. No ocean, eh? But the beach—fine! Keep out in the air; keep out in the sunshine. Do you more good than a lot of foolish medicine."

So Jackie went to the beach that morning as usual. John and Marian slept till one o'clock. Then John, after luncheon, drove off in the car to keep a tennis engagement. "Promised Sally last night I'd play doubles. . . ."

Marian shouted after him some casual sporting benediction. She was in her room, dressing. She herself had a date that afternoon with Tom. He would arrive shortly in *his* car, and they would drive out to the rocks at Devil's Cove. . . . She laughed suddenly at the patent absurdity of this exchange, this almost formal, almost mechanical transfer of interests. Her husband rushing off to play with Sally, and Sally's

husband rushing off to play with her! How unutterably
childish! Yet all the time she was making herself as
attractive as possible, putting on her smartest sport
skirt, her gayest colored sweater, her most fetching
hat—the yellow straw with the sprig of artificial wheat
aslant the crown. . . .

Tom Nevinson arrived: a solid, rather boisterous
young gallant in white flannels and a tweed jacket,
who smoked an incongruous, delicate-looking briar
pipe.

She listened all the way to Devil's Cove to his breezy
protestations of passion. He was not (he said) the
sort of poor fish who went around making love to
every woman he met. Not much! Of course in his
college days (this with a sigh) he'd been—well, the
usual sort of indiscriminate young fool. But he'd
learned by bitter experience the value of true emotion.
And of course he cared a lot for Sally, just as she,
Marian, cared a lot about John. . . . Why, sure!
He understood all that. But life was so short and, er—
it was all such a queer jumble, that—well—it seemed
just a darned shame not to be honest and speak out
when you met someone who really meant something
to you.

"But that's such an obvious sort of truth," said
Marian. "Such an old truth! And—forgive me—
such an unsubstantial one. I want something more
from you, Tom."

"Something more?" He was puzzled, curious, wondering whether he dared assume that she was deliberately tempting him. . . .

"Yes. You don't happen to have any sort of *divine*
truth concealed about your person, do you?"

"Any sort of what? Divine truth? Are you kidding me, my beautiful?"

"I am not."

"Well, then, I don't get you."

"All right," said Marian serenely.

"My dear girl—"

She stopped him with a quick dart of her hand toward his arm.

"Take me home, Tom."

"Not yet, Marian! Don't spoil things. This is our day, our moment—"

He drew her to him. The delicate-looking pipe was removed, with a gesture, from his lips. . . . He kissed her, and she made no protest. She made no comment whatsoever.

She simply got up and started toward the car. He followed her.

"Marian dearest—"

"I must get home, Tom. You've got to take me. Something's happening! Something dreadful's happening— And please—drive fast!"

But when she got home she found that her fear— the black fear that had seized her so unreasonably— was without justification in fact. Miss Mosby, to be sure, reported that Jackie had a little fever.

Marian nodded and went into the nursery.

"Well, Jackie boy, how do you feel?"

"Fine, Mother."

"You must keep covered up. . . . You'll be all right to-morrow. . . . Do you know who's in the living-room?"

"Mr. Nevinson," guessed Jackie, with devastating promptness.

"Yes, he is. . . . But I mean—I meant some-one else. A friend of yours!"

"I don't know."

"Mr. Onion! He's standing up on top of the book-shelves—"

"Oh, yes," said Jackie. "He likes it up there."

"But—shan't I bring him to you?"

"No matter. Because Mr. Onion has to stay there for a special reason. Because if any giants or dragons come in he can see them and then he can climb down and hit them with his ladder and they'll be dead."

"Darling! Where do you get these extraordinary ideas—!"

"There's a dragon 'at lives under the house. Mr. Onion saw him, and he was all black, like when you shut your eyes tight, and Mr. Onion says he might come down the chimney—"

"Jackie! Listen to Mother! There *aren't* any giants or dragons—" blundered Marian; but she was not so sure. Jackie's faintly superior smile made her doubt the rationalistic hypothesis. . . . She leaned down and kissed him. "Blessed baby!" she murmured; and again was strangely humbled by his smile.

Returning to the living-room, she found not only Tom but also Sally and John and several others—all members of the crowd—gathered for cocktails. John was doing the honors. As she came in she caught his eye, and for an instant he stood rigid, with the cock-tail shaker poised like a gleaming piston at the top of its stroke. "Anything wrong?" his raised eyebrows telegraphed her. She didn't answer. She couldn't. The moment dragged out and grew thin—grew taut as a stretched fiddle string.

The others felt this tension. Sally Nevinson had been kidding Tom about the extravagant tie he'd put on for his date with Marian. "I can always tell when Tom's hard hit. . . . His tie gives him away. . . . It's an emotional barometer. . . ." But suddenly her shrill voice broke. . . . She whirled and stared at Marian. "Good Lord!" She flung out. "What's the matter? You look as tho you'd been seeing things!"

"I have," said Marian.

John stepped forward quickly. "What is it?" he asked.

"It's a dragon that lives under the house," replied Marian, and laughed. "Jackie's been telling me about it. . . . Give me a drink, will you, John dear? I need it for my nerves. . . . You see, I'm scared of the dragon."

Her laugh somehow destroyed the charm of the cocktail hour. People drifted away. . . . John and Marian were left alone. "Tell me," he said.

"There's nothing to tell."

"Yes, there is. You know there is! Is it Tom? Is it Sally? Is it—Jackie."

She shook her head.

"It's nothing I can put into words. It's just a feeling. A dragon under the house—"

"What's all this nonsense about a dragon?"

"It's black," said Marian.

"Gosh!" he muttered. "You're getting beyond me, old girl! I can't make you out half the time—"

"Then ask Mr. Onion!" cried Marian, pointing to the little figure on the bookshelves. "He understands—"

"What you need is sleep," decided John. "We'll

cut out that dance at the country club to-night. Go
to bed early. Get a good night's rest—"

It was well that they did go to bed early that
night, for at three o'clock in the morning Miss Mosby
woke them to say that Jackie was very ill. He had
a temperature of 103 and was breathing hard. He
was also coughing a good deal.

"I've already telephoned for the doctor," said the
efficient Miss Mosby as Marian struggled into kimono
and bedroom slippers. To John, plunging in from the
sleeping porch, she said: "You had better put on your
heavy dressing gown, Mr. Thurston. There's a chill
in the air this morning."

A chill in the air, thought Marian. A dragon under
the house. . . . So many things that can't be put
into words. . . .

Then it all came down to one word; to one dreadful,
ominous word that was like a weight on your heart:

Pneumonia.

Dr. Moulton, the tall, kindly, capable country doctor
who had ministered to Jackie's minor summer ailments
since he was born, was the first to utter this word.
He said it gravely, simply, as one who knows the im-
possibility of cheating life with accents and inflections.
. . . Later, the next afternoon, it was repeated
by a locally famous physician, Dr. Hurd, whom Moulton had summoned from Portland. . . . Also from
Portland arrived a trained nurse. Miss Mosby hated
her on sight. . . .

For three days little Jackie's life hung in the balance.
Then at noon of the fourth day Dr. Moulton said to
Marian: "We're doin' all we can for the boy, Mrs.
Thurston. But I must tell you the truth. It looks

pretty bad right now. If there's anybody else you'd
like to call in—"

Marian—the ghost of Marian—went straight to the
ghost of her husband, John.

"I want the greatest in the country," she said.
"There must be some one specialist. . . . Not that
I believe he can do any more than they've done. But
just because he *is* the greatest. . . ."

John nodded and went to the telephone. For more
than an hour he invoked, with the meticulous patience
of despair, various distant persons—beings—disem-
bodied voices. Then five minutes of sharp, brisk, businesslike conversation, and the thing was done.

"Dr. Vance," he mumbled to Marian, wiping the
sweat from his face, "leaves New York to-night on the
State of Maine, arrives five-forty to-morrow morning.
I mustn't forget to have a car at the station to meet
him."

"To-morrow morning may be too late," said Marian,
in the queer, hushed voice that had been her voice for
the past four days. "If only we had someone here
now. . . . If only we had some God to pray to.
We have no God—"

Then John cried out, a deep, guttural cry that
came from the depths of his tortured soul.

"No! We haven't! And I refuse to fake one!"

"I would if I could," said Marian. "But I can't.
I've tried, and I can't—"

Toward morning they called her. She went into
Jackie's room. Dr. Moulton and Dr. Hurd were
standing together by the bed. The nurse whom Miss
Mosby hated made a pale figure against the wall, and
Miss Mosby herself was in the doorway. There was a

faint light from the window; a gray hint of
dawn. . . .

Marian leaned over her son. Her pose, the ma-
ternal brooding of her body, the soft fall of her hands
against the mounded bedclothes, served to banish the
professional restraint of the sickroom. And when she
spoke her simple question seemed somehow to tran-
scend its own scientific futility.

"Jackie darling, aren't you ever going to get well?"

The small figure stirred. It stirred. Then the child's
voice came reluctantly—so frail an answer, so light a
thread that Marian's heart almost stopped beating.

"I don't know. . . . Mother. . . . You'll
have to ask. . . . Mr. Onion. . . ."

She straightened up at once. Miss Mosby, in the
doorway, stood aside to let her pass. Miss Mosby
thought that Mrs. Thurston was smiling, but she
could not be sure. One could not be sure of anything
just then.

Marian walked blindly through the silent house to
the door of the living-room. There she stopped, aware
of some happening that must not be disturbed; aware
of something going on in the twilight of that many-
windowed room: a sort of birth, a revelation and a
renascence that offered high defiance to the pervading
thrust of death.

A figure was kneeling before the bookshelves. She
knew, of course, that it was John, but the familiar
sense of him as flesh and blood was so dimmed by the
uncertain light that only his pose mattered. It alone
had substance, and that substance was so strange, so
blurred with beauty, that she almost cried out in rap-
ture. Then she heard his voice and she knew that
he was praying.

"Listen, Mr. Onion, don't let him die. Save him, save Jackie. . . . Mr. Onion. . . . He loves you. That makes you alive. He believes in you. That makes you divine. . . . Listen, you've got to! He believes in you. You're his great treasure. You're the wonder of his life. I love him too, but my love isn't enough. . . . Because I've never been more to him than his father. . . . I've never given him magic. . . . I've never given him wonder. . . . Oh, Mr. Onion. . . . Mr. Onion! Oh, God. . . . Save him. . . . I ask you on my knees. . . . I pray to you—"

The strangely articulate, strangely broken voice went on like a groping music that hadn't quite learned to be music. And the light creeping up the hill and warming the windows was like a mute response. . . . Marian turned and ran, sure-footed among shadowy pieces of furniture, among shadowy fears, back to the nursery. The two doctors now were leaning over the bed, but she paid no attention to them. She too leaned down; she would remember this bending of her body all her life long. . . .

"Jackie! Can you hear me?"

The frail voice replied after an interval: "Yes, Mother."

"Then—listen, darling! I asked—Daddy asked Mr. Onion if you were going to get well, and Mr. Onion said 'Yes.' He said—you were to try very hard and then you'd get well—"

"Mr. Onion said—?"

"That it was all right! That you were going to get well!" There was a moment of absolute stillness. Then Jackie sighed—a faint, far sigh of reassurance, of childish contentment and peace. Then, turning on his side, he nestled down comfortably to sleep.

A moment later Marian heard the crunch of car wheels on the drive outside the house and knew that Dr. Vance, the great specialist, had arrived. But she knew also that he was only another lay figure, another supernumerary in the transpired drama that could not be put into words; that could never be put into words. . . .

Dr. Vance appeared, puffing. He was a little, round, fussy man who waddled in and looked at Jackie, and said: "Ah! Hum! Indeed!" and waddled out again, with John and Marian tagging at his heels.

"I want some breakfast. Angels in heaven, what a train! *What* a train! I want some coffee. With hot milk and no sugar. And three eggs boiled four minutes by the clock. By the clock, mind you! I'm very particular about my eggs."

"Jackie!" blurted out John, with a racked smile. "What about Jackie?"

"Going to get well. Well now. Keep him warm. Keep the windows open. Of *course!* Healthy youngster. Good air. *Bound* to pull through. Ask your doctors. I'm not a doctor. I'm a traveling man. Cost you five hundred dollars. Highway robbery. Can't help it. Must keep people in awe of specialists. Only way to do it is to overcharge them. If you have an old-fashioned coffeepot, I prefer it to the modern percolator. And I like my toast just a little bit burned at the edges. . . ."

An hour later John and Marian were sitting on the bench at the edge of the hill, facing the sea. Their bodies a little apart, their hands not touching, they experienced nevertheless that knowledge of each other, that sense of contact which is marriage rarely realized.

"So I prayed," said John. "I had to. If it was cowardice, then it was cowardice. But I had to."

"I know . . . heard you. . . . I came to the door while you were kneeling there. . . ."

"Funny thing," he said.

"Beautiful thing," said Marian.

"It was real. That's what I mean. And—it's going to make a difference. Can't go on living as we have been. . . . Do the same things, maybe. But there'll be a new element in everything. . . . Always a new element. . . . Only I suspect it's old . . . old and—indispensable. The element of search—man searching for the source of his wonder, man searching for his God. . . ."

"That's what I tried to say to you the other day, the other morning."

"It can't be said," replied John. "It can never be said. Because there's no guide to the search and no definition for the thing found. There's only the necessity—I felt that last night—for man to go beyond himself, to go beyond reason, even beyond truth, as Jackie's young mind went beyond the truth of Mr. Onion. . . . Mr. Onion can be explained, but Jackie's thought of him can never be explained . . . but somewhere along the path of that thought is the power and the glory. . . ."

"We can never tell anyone," said Marian. "This is our secret, and this is . . . our wedding day."

"Happy is the bride the sun shines on," said John.

A HORSEMAN IN THE SKY

By Ambrose Bierce

Chapter I

One sunny afternoon in the autumn of the year 1861 a soldier lay in a clump of laurel by the side of a road in western Virginia. He lay at full length upon his stomach, his feet resting upon the toes, his head upon the left forearm. His extended right hand loosely grasped his rifle. But for the somewhat methodical disposition of his limbs and a slight rhythmic movement of the cartridge-box at the back of his belt he might have been thought to be dead. He was asleep at his post of duty. But if detected he would be dead shortly afterward, death being the just and legal penalty of his crime.

The lump of laurel in which the criminal lay was in the angle of a road which after ascending southward a steep acclivity to that point turned sharply to the west, running along the summit for perhaps one hundred yards. There it turned southward again and went zigzagging downward through the forest. At the salient of that second angle was a large flat rock, jutting out northward, overlooking the deep valley from which the road ascended. The rock capped a high cliff; a stone dropped from its outer edge would have fallen sheer downward one thousand feet to the tops of the pines. The angle where the soldier lay was on another spur of the same cliff. Had he been awake he would have commanded a view, not only of the short arm of the road and the jutting rock, but of the entire profile of the cliff below it. It might well have made him giddy to look.

The country was wooded everywhere except at the bottom of the valley to the northward, where there was a small natural meadow, through which flowed a stream scarcely visible from the valley's rim. This open ground looked hardly larger than an ordinary door-yard, but was really several acres in extent. Its green was more vivid than that of the inclosing forest. Away beyond it rose a line of giant cliffs similar to those upon which we are supposed to stand in our survey of the savage scene, and through which the road had somehow made its climb to the summit. The configuration of the valley, indeed, was such that from this point of observation it seemed entirely shut in, and one could but have wondered how the road which found a way out of it had found a way into it, and whence came and whither went the waters of the stream that parted the meadow more than a thousand feet below.

No country is so wild and difficult but men will make it a theater of war; concealed in the forest at the bottom of that military rat-trap, in which half a hundred men in possession of the exits might have starved an army to submission, lay five regiments of Federal infantry. They had marched all the previous day and night and were resting. At nightfall they would take to the road again, climb to the place where their unfaithful sentinel now slept, and descending the other slope of the ridge fall upon a camp of the enemy at about midnight. Their hope was to surprise it, for the road led to the rear of it. In case of failure, their position would be perilous in the extreme; and fail they surely would should accident or vigilance apprize the enemy of the movement.

Chapter II

The sleeping sentinel in the clump of laurel was a young Virginian named Carter Druse. He was the son of wealthy parents, an only child, and had known such ease and cultivation and high living as wealth and taste were able to command in the mountain country of western Virginia. His home was but a few miles from where he now lay. One morning he had risen from the breakfast-table and said, quietly but gravely: "Father, a Union regiment has arrived at Grafton. I am going to join it."

The father lifted his leonine head, looked at the son a moment in silence, and replied; "Well, go, sir, and whatever may occur do what you conceive to be your duty. Virginia, to which you are a traitor, must get on without you. Should we both live to the end of the war, we will speak further of the matter. Your mother, as the physician has informed you, is in a most critical condition; at the best she cannot be with us longer than a few weeks, but that time is precious. It would be better not to disturb her."

So Carter Druse, bowing reverently to his father, who returned the salute with a stately courtesy that masked a breaking heart, left the home of his childhood to go soldiering. By conscience and courage, by deeds of devotion and daring, he soon commended himself to his fellows and his officers; and it was to these

qualities and to some knowledge of the country that
he owed his selection for his present perilous duty at
the extreme outpost. Nevertheless, fatigue had been
stronger than resolution and he had fallen asleep. What
good or bad angel came in a dream to rouse him from
his state of crime, who shall say? Without a movement, without a sound, in the profound silence and the
languor of the late afternoon, some invisible messenger
of fate touched with unsealing finger the eyes of his
consciousness—whispered into the ear of his spirit the
mysterious awakening word which no human lips ever
have spoken, no human memory ever has recalled. He
quietly raised his forehead from his arm and looked
between the masking stems of the laurels, instinctively
closing his right hand about the stock of his rifle.

His first feeling was a keen artistic delight. On a
colossal pedestal, the cliff,—motionless at the extreme
edge of the capping rock and sharply outlined against
the sky,—was an equestrian statue of impressive
dignity. The figure of the man sat the figure of the
horse, straight and soldierly, but with the repose of a
Grecian god carved in the marble which limits the
suggestion of activity. The gray costume harmonized
with its aerial background; the metal of accouterment
and caparison was softened and subdued by the
shadow; the animal's skin had no points of high
light. A carbine strikingly foreshortened lay across
the pommel of the saddle, kept in place by the right
hand grasping it at the "grip"; the left hand, holding
the bridle rein, was invisible. In silhouette against the
sky the profile of the horse was cut with the sharpness
of a cameo; it looked across the heights of air to the
confronting cliffs beyond. The face of the rider,
turned slightly away, showed only an outline of temple

and beard; he was looking downward to the bottom of the valley. Magnified by its lift against the sky and by the soldier's testifying sense of the formidableness of a near enemy the group appeared of heroic, almost colossal, size.

For an instant Druse had a strange, half-defined feeling that he had slept to the end of the war and was looking upon a noble work of art reared upon that eminence to commemorate the deeds of an heroic past of which he had been an inglorious part. The feeling was dispelled by a· slight movement of the group: the horse, without moving its feet, had drawn its body slightly backward from the verge; the man remained immobile as before. Broad awake and keenly alive to the significance of the situation, Druse now brought the butt of his rifle against his cheek by cautiously pushing the barrel forward through the bushes, cocked the piece, and glancing through the sights covered a vital spot of the horseman's breast. A touch upon the trigger and all would have been well with Carter Druse. At that instant the horseman turned his head and looked in the direction of his concealed foeman—seemed to look into his very face, into his eyes, into his brave, compassionate heart.

Is it then so terrible to kill an enemy in war—an enemy who has surprized a secret vital to the safety of one's self and comrades—an enemy more formidable for his knowledge than all his army for its numbers? Carter Druse grew pale; he shook in every limb, turned faint, and saw the statuesque group before him as black figures, rising, falling, moving unsteadily in arcs of circles in a fiery sky. His hand fell away from his weapon, his head slowly dropped until his face rested on the leaves in which he lay. This courageous gentleman and hardy soldier was near swooning from intensity of emotion.

It was not for long; in another moment his face was raised from earth, his hands resumed their places on the rifle, his forefinger sought the trigger; mind, heart, and eyes were clear, conscience and reason sound. He could not hope to capture that enemy; to alarm him would but send him dashing to his camp with his fatal news. The duty of the soldier was plain: the man must be shot dead from ambush— without warning, without a moment's spiritual preparation, with never so much as an unspoken prayer, he must be sent to his account. But no—there is a hope; he may have discovered nothing—perhaps he is but admiring the sublimity of the landscape. If permitted, he may turn and ride carelessly away in the direction whence he came. Surely it will be possible to judge at the instant of his withdrawing whether he knows. It may well be that his fixity of attention—Druse turned his head and looked through the deeps of air downward, as from the surface to the bottom of a translucent sea. He saw creeping across the green meadow a sinuous line of figures of men and horses— some foolish commander was permitting the soldiers of his escort to water their beasts in the open, in plain view from a dozen summits!

Druse withdrew his eyes from the valley and fixed them again upon the group of man and horse in the sky, and again it was through the sights of his rifle. But this time his aim was at the horse. In his memory, as if they were a divine mandate, rang the words of his father at their parting: "Whatever may occur, do what you conceive to be your duty." He was calm now. His teeth were firmly but not rigidly closed;

his nerves were as tranquil as a sleeping babe's—not a tremor affected any muscle of his body; his breathing, until suspended in the act of taking aim, was regular and slow. Duty had conquered; the spirit had said to the body: "Peace, be still." He fired.

Chapter III

An officer of the Federal force, who in a spirit of adventure or in quest of knowledge had left the hidden *bivouac* in the valley, and with aimless feet had made his way to the lower edge of a small open space near the foot of the cliff, was considering what he had to gain by pushing his exploration further. At a distance of a quarter-mile before him, but apparently at a stone's throw, rose from its fringe of pines the gigantic face of rock, towering to so great a height above him that it made him giddy to look up to where its edge cut a sharp, rugged line against the sky. It presented a clean, vertical profile against a background of blue sky to a point half the way down, and of distant hills, hardly less blue, thence to the tops of the trees at its base. Lifting his eyes to the dizzy altitude of its summit the officer saw an astonishing sight—a man on horseback riding down into the valley through the air!

Straight upright sat the rider, in military fashion, with a firm seat in the saddle, a strong clutch upon the rein to hold his charger from too impetuous a plunge. From his bare head his long hair streamed upward, waving like a plume. His hands were concealed in the cloud of the horse's lifted mane. The animal's body was as level as if every hoof-stroke encountered the resistant earth. Its motions were those of a wild gallop, but even as the officer looked they ceased, with all the legs thrown sharply forward as in the act of alighting from a leap. But this was a flight!

Filled with amazement and terror by this apparition of a horseman in the sky—half believing himself the chosen scribe of some new Apocalypse, the officer was overcome by the intensity of his emotions; his legs failed him and he fell. Almost at the same instant he heard a crashing sound in the trees—a sound that died without an echo—and all was still.

The officer rose to his feet, trembling. The familiar sensation of an abraded shin recalled his dazed faculties. Pulling himself together he ran rapidly obliquely away from the cliff to a point distant from its foot; thereabout he expected to find his man; and thereabout he naturally failed. In the fleeting instant of his vision his imagination had been so wrought upon by the apparent grace and ease and intention of the marvelous performance that it did not occur to him that the line of march of aerial cavalry is directly downward, and that he could find the objects of his search at the very foot of the cliff. A half-hour later he returned to camp.

This officer was a wise man; he knew better than to tell an incredible truth. He said nothing of what he had seen. But when the commander asked him if in his scout he had learned anything of advantage to the expedition he answered:

"Yes, sir; there is no road leading down into this valley from the southward."

The commander, knowing better, smiled.

Chapter IV

After firing his shot, Private Carter Druse reloaded his rifle and resumed his watch. Ten minutes had hardly passed when a Federal sergeant crept cautiously to him on hands and knees. Druse neither turned his head nor looked at him, but lay without motion or sign of recognition.

"Did you fire?" the sergeant whispered.

"Yes."

"At what?"

"A horse. It was standing on yonder rock—pretty far out. You see it is no longer there. It went over the cliff."

The man's face was white, but he showed no other sign of emotion. Having answered, he turned away his eyes and said no more. The sergeant did not understand.

"See here, Druse," he said, after a moment's silence, "it's no use making a mystery. I order you to report. Was there anybody on the horse?"

"Yes."

"Well?"

"My father."

The sergeant rose to his feet and walked away. "Good God!" he said.

THE AGE FOR LOVE

By Paul Bourget

When I submitted the plan of my Inquiry Upon the Age for Love to the editor-in-chief of the Boulevard, the highest type of French literary paper, he seemed astonished that an idea so journalistic—that was his word—should have been evolved from the brain of his most recent acquisition. I had been with him two weeks and it was my first contribution. "Give me some details, my dear Labarthe," he said, in a somewhat less insolent manner than was his wont. After listening to me for a few moments he conti-ued: "That is good. You will go and interview certain men and women, first upon the age at which one loves the most, next upon the age when one is mos loved? Is that your idea? And now to whom will you go first?"

"I have prepared a list," I replied and took from my pocket a sheet of paper. I had jotted down the names of a number of celebrities whom I proposed to interview on this all-important question, and I began to read over my list. It contained two ex-government officials, a general, a Dominican father, four actresses, two café-concert singers, four actors, two financiers, two lawyers, a surgeon and a lot of literary celebrities. At some of the names my chief would nod his approval, at others he would say curtly, with an affectation of American manners, "Bad; strike it off," until I came to the name I had kept for the last, that of Pierre Fauchery, the famous novelist.

"Strike that off," he said, shrugging his shoulders. "He is not on good terms with us."

"And yet," I suggested, "is there any one whose opinion would be of greater interest to reading men as well as to women? I had even thought of beginning with him."

"The devil you had!" interrupted the editor-in-chief. "It is one of Fauchery's principles not to see any reporters. I have sent him ten if I have one, and he has shown them all the door. The Boulevard does not relish such treatment, so we have given him some pretty hard hits."

"Nevertheless, I will have an interview with Fauchery for the Boulevard," was my reply. "I am sure of it."

"If you succeed," he replied, "I'll raise your salary. That man makes me tired with his scorn of newspaper notoriety. He must take his share of it, like the rest. But you will not succeed. What makes you think you can?"

"Permit me to tell you my reason later. In forty-eight hours you will see whether I have succeeded or not."

"Go and do not spare the fellow."

Decidedly. I had made some progress as a journalist, even in my two weeks' apprenticeship, if I could permit Pascal to speak in this way of the man I most admired among living writers. Since that not far-distant time when, tired of being poor, I had made up my mind to cast my lot with the multitude in Paris, I had tried to lay aside my old self, as lizards do their skins, and I had almost succeeded. In a former time, a former time that was but yesterday, I knew—for in a drawer full of poems, dramas and half-finished

tales I had proof of it—that there had once existed
a certain Jules Labarthe who had come to Paris with
the hope of becoming a great man. That person
believed in Literature with a capital "L" in the Ideal,
another capital; in Glory, a third capital. He was now
dead and buried. Would he some day, his position
assured, begin to write once more from pure love of
his art? Possibly, but for the moment I knew only
the energetic, practical Labarthe, who had joined the
procession with the idea of getting into the front
rank, and of obtaining as soon as possible an income
of thirty thousand francs a year. What would it
matter to this second individual if that vile Pascal
should boast of having stolen a march on the most delicate, the most powerful of the heirs of Balzac, since
I, the new Labarthe, was capable of looking forward
to an operation which required about as much delicacy as some of the performances of my editor-in-
chief? I had, as a matter of fact, a sure means of
obtaining the interview. It was this: When I was
young and simple I had sent some verses and stories
to Pierre Fauchery, the same verses and stories the
refusal of which by four editors had finally made me
decide to enter the field of journalism. The great
writer was traveling at this time, but he had replied
to me. I had responded by a letter to which he again
replied, this time with an invitation to call upon him.
I went. I did not find him. I went again. I did not
find him that time. Then a sort of timidity prevented my
returning to the charge. So I had never met him. He
knew me only as the young Elia of my two epistles.
This is what I counted upon to extort from him the
favor of an interview which he certainly would refuse
to a mere newspaper man. My plan was simple; to

present myself at his house, to be received, to conceal
my real occupation, to sketch vaguely a subject for a
novel in which there should occur a discussion upon the
Age for Love, to make him talk and then when he
should discover his conversation in print—here I
began to feel some remorse. But I stifled it with the
terrible phrase, "the struggle for life," and also by the
recollection of numerous examples culled from the firm
with which I now had the honor of being connected.

The morning after I had had this very literary conversation with my honorable director, I rang at the
door of the small house in the Rue Desbordes-Valmore
where Pierre Fauchery lived, in a retired corner of
Passy. Having taken up my pen to tell a plain unvar-
nished tale I do not see how I can conceal the wretched
feeling of pleasure which, as I rang the bell, warmed
my heart at the thought of the good joke I was about
to play on the owner of this peaceful abode.

Even after making up one's mind to the sacrifices
I had decided upon, there is always left a trace of
envy for those who have triumphed in the melancholy
        for literary supremacy. It was a real dis-
                    the servant replied, ill-humor-
                    as not in Paris. I asked
                    e servant did not know.
                    e servant did not know
                    he had secured anonymity
                    r later I had discovered
                    present at the Château de
                    had merely had to make
                    Two hours later I bought
                    de Lyon for the little town
                    e scene for his delicious story
                    took a traveling bag and was

prepared to spend the night there. In case I failed
to see the master that afternoon I had decided to make
sure of him the next morning. Exactly seven hours
after the servant, faithful to his trust, had declared
that he did not know where his master was staying, I
was standing in the hall of the château waiting for my
card to be sent up. I had taken care to write on it
a reminder of our conversation of the year before,
and this time, after a ten-minute wait in the hall, during which I noticed with singular curiosity and *malice*
two very elegant and very pretty young women going
out for a walk, I was admitted to his presence. "Aha,"
I said to myself, "this then is the secret of his exile;
the interview promises well!"

The novelist received me in a cosy little room,
with a window opening onto the park, already beginning to turn yellow with the advancing autumn.
A wood fire burned in the fireplace and lighted up the
walls which were hung with flowered cretonne and on
which could be distinguished several colored English
prints representing cross-country rides and the ju
ing of hedges. Here was the worldly environ
which Fauchery is so often re
and papers that littered th
the present occupant of th
a substantial man of l
work was still further a
admit, gave me all at on
the trick I was about to
him the snobbish pretend
papers were in the habit of
been a delight to outwit his
saw, as he put down his pen
about fifty-seven years old, w

the marks of reflection, eyes tired from sleeplessness, a brow heavy with thought, who said as he pointed to an easy chair, "You will excuse me, my dear confrère, for keeping you waiting." I, his dear confrère! Ah! if he had known! "You see," and he pointed to the page still wet with ink, "that man cannot be free from the slavery of furnishing copy. One has less facility at my age than at yours. Now, let us speak of yourself. How do you happen to be at Nemours? What have you been doing since the story and the verses you were kind enough to send me?"

It is vain to try to sacrifice once for all one's youthful ideals. When a man has loved literature as I loved it at twenty, he cannot be satisfied at twenty-six to give up his early passion, even at the bidding of implacable necessity. So Pierre Fauchery remembered my poor verses! He had actually read my story! His allusion proved it. Could I tell him at such a moment that since the creation of those first works I had despaired of myself, and that I had changed my gun to the other shoulder? The image of the Boulevard office rose suddenly before me. I heard the voice of the editor-in-chief saying, "Interview Fauchery? You will never accomplish that"; so, faithful to my self-imposed rôle, I replied, "I have retired to Nemours to work upon a novel called The Age for Love, and it is on this subject that I wished to consult you, my dear master."

It seemed to me—it may possibly have been an illusion—that at the announcement of the so-called title of my so-called novel, a smile and a shadow flitted over Fauchery's eyes and mouth. A vision of the two young women I had met in the hall came back to me. Was the author of so many great masterpieces of analysis about to live a new book before writing it? I had no time to answer this question, for, with a glance at an onyx vase containing some cigarets of Turkish tobacco, he offered me one, lighted one himself and began first to question, then to reply to me. I listened while he thought aloud and had almost forgotten my Machiavellian combination, so keen was my relish of the joyous intimacy of this communion with a mind I had passionately loved in his works. He was the first of the great writers of our day whom I had thus approached on something like terms of intimacy. As we talked I observed the strange similarity between his spoken and his written words. I admired the charming simplicity with which he abandoned himself to the pleasures of imagination, his superabundant intelligence, the liveliness of his impressions and his total absence of arrogance and of pose.

"There is no such thing as an age for love," he said in substance, "because the man capable of loving— in the complex and modern sense of love as a sort of ideal exaltation—never ceases to love. I will go further; he never ceases to love the same person. You know the experiment that a contemporary physiologist tried with a series of portraits to determine in what the indefinable resemblances called family likeness consisted? He took photographs of twenty persons of the same blood, then he photographed these photographs on the same plate, one over the other. In this way he discovered the common features which determined the type. Well, I am convinced that if we could try a similar experiment and photograph one upon another the pictures of the different women whom the same man has loved or thought he had loved in the course of his life we should discover that all these women resembled one another. The most inconsistent have cherished one and the same being through five or six or even twenty different embodiments. The main point is to find out at what age they have met the woman who approaches nearest to the one whose image they have constantly borne within themselves. For them that would be the age for love.

"The age for being loved?" he continued. "The deepest of all the passions I have ever known a man to inspire was in the case of one of my masters, a poet, and he was sixty years old at the time. It is true that he still held himself as erect as a young man, he came and went with a step as light as yours, he conversed like Rivarol, he composed verses as beautiful as De Vigny's. He was besides very poor, very lonely and very unhappy, having lost one after another, his wife and his children. You remember the words of Shakespeare's Moor: 'She loved me for the dangers I had passed, and I loved her that she did pity them.'

"So it was that this great artist inspired in a beautiful, noble and wealthy young Russian woman, a devotion so passionate that because of him she never married. She found a way to take care of him, day and night, in spite of his family, during his last illness, and at the present time, having bought from his heirs all of the poet's personal belongings, she keeps the apartment where he lived just as it was at the time of his death. That was years ago. In her case she found in a man three times her own age the person who corresponded to a certain ideal which she carried in her heart. Look at Goethe, at Lamartine and at many others! To depict feelings on this high plane, you must give up the process of minute and insignificant observation which is the bane of the artists of to-day.

In order that a sixty-year-old lover should appear
neither ridiculous nor odious you must apply to him
what the elder Corneille so proudly said of himself
in his lines to the marquise:

> "'Cependant, 'jai quelques charmes
> Qui sont assez eclatants
> Pour n'avoir pas trop d'alarmes
> De ces ravages du temps.'

"Have the courage to analyze great emotions, to
create characters who shall be lofty and true. The
whole art of the analytical novel lies there."

As he spoke the master had such a light of intellec-
tual certainty in his eyes that to me he seemed the
embodiment of one of those great characters he had
been urging me to describe. It made me feel that
the theory of this man, himself almost a sexagenarian,
that at any age one may inspire love, was not unrea-
sonable! The contrast between the world of ideas in
which he moved and the atmosphere of the literary
shop in which for the last few months I had been
stifling was too strong. The dreams of my youth were
realized in this man whose gifts remained unimpaired
after the production of thirty volumes and whose face,
growing old, was a living illustration of the beautiful
saying: "Since we must wear out, let us wear out
nobly." His slender figure bespoke the austerity of
long hours of work; his firm mouth showed his de-
cision of character; his brow, with its deep furrows,
had the paleness of the paper over which he so often
bent; and yet, the refinement of his hands, so well
cared for, the sober elegance of his dress and an aristo-
cratic air that was natural to him showed that the finer
professional virtues had been cultivated in the midst
of a life of frivolous temptations. These temptations

had been no more of a disturbance to his ethical and
spiritual nature than the academic honors, the financial
successes, the numerous editions that had been his.
Withal he was an awfully good fellow, for, after
having talked at great length with me, he ended
by saying, "Since you are staying in Nemours I hope
to see you often, and to-day I cannot let you go without presenting you to my hostess."

What could I say? This was the way in which
a mere reporter on the Boulevard found himself installed at a five-o'clock tea-table in the salon of a
château, where surely no newspaper man had ever
before set foot and was presented as a young poet and
novelist of the future to the old Marquise de Proby,
whose guest the master was. This amiable white-
haired dowager questioned me upon my alleged work
and I replied equivocally, with blushes, which the good
lady must have attributed to bashful timidity. Then,
as tho some evil genius had conspired to multiply the
witnesses of my bad conduct, the two young women
whom I had seen going out, returned in the midst of
my unlooked-for visit. Ah, my interview with this
student of femininity upon the Age for Love was about
to have a living commentary! How it would illumine
his words to hear him conversing with these new
arrivals! One was a young girl of possibly twenty—
a Russian if I rightly understood the name. She
was rather tall, with a long face lighted up by two very
gentle black eyes, singular in their fire and intensity.
She bore a striking resemblance to the portrait attributed to Francia in the Salon Carré of the Louvre which
goes by the name of the "Man in Black," because of
the color of his clothes and his mantle. About her
mouth and nostrils was that same subdued nervousness,

that same restrained feverishness which gives to the portrait its striking qualities. I had not been there a quarter of an hour before I had guessed from the way she watched and listened to Fauchery what a passionate interest the old master inspired in her. When he spoke she paid rapt attention. When she spoke to him, I felt her voice shiver, if I may use the word, and he, the glorious writer, surfeited with triumphs, exhausted by his labors, seemed, as soon as he felt the radiance of her glance of ingenuous idolatry, to recover that vivacity, that elasticity of impression, which is the sovereign grace of youthful lovers.

"I understand now why he cited Goethe and the young girl of Marienbad," said I to myself with a laugh, as my hired carriage sped on toward Nemours. "He was thinking of himself. He is in love with that child, and she is in love with him. We shall hear of his marrying her. There's a wedding that will call forth copy, and when Pascal hears that I witnessed the courtship—but just now I must think of my interview. Won't Fauchery be surprised to read it day after to-morrow in his paper? But does he read the papers? It may not be right, but what harm will it do him? Besides, it's a part of the struggle for life." It was by such reasoning, I remember, the reasoning of a man determined to arrive, that I tried to lull to sleep the inward voice that cried, "You have no right to put on paper, to give to the public, what this noble writer said to you, supposing that he was receiving a poet, not a reporter." But I heard also the voice of my chief saying, "You will never succeed." And this second voice, I am ashamed to confess, triumphed over the other with all the more ease because I was obliged to do something to kill time. I reached Ne-

mours too late for the train which would have brought
me back to Paris about dinner time. At the old
inn they gave me a room which was clean and quiet,
a good place to write, so I spent the evening until
bedtime composing the first of the articles which were
to form my inquiry. I scribbled away under the
vivid impressions of the afternoon, my powers as well
as my nerves spurred by a touch of remorse. Yes, I
scribbled four pages which would have been no dis-
grace to the Journal des Goncourts, that exquisite
manual of the perfect reporter. It was all there,
my journey, my arrival at the château, a sketch of
the quaint eighteenth century building, with its fringe
of trees and its well-kept walks, the master's room, the
master himself and his conversation; the tea at the
end and the smile of the old novelist in the midst of a
circle of admirers, old and young. It lacked only a
few closing lines. "I will add these in the morning."
I thought, and went to bed with a feeling of duty
performed, such is the nature of a writer. Under the
form of an interview I had done, and I knew it, the
best work of my life.

What happens while we sleep? Is there, unknown
to us, a secret and irresistible ferment of ideas while
our senses are closed to the impressions of the outside
world? Certain it is that on awakening I am apt to
find myself in a state of mind very different from that
in which I went to sleep. I had not been awake ten
minutes before the image of Pierre Fauchery came up
before me, and at the same time the thought that I
had taken a base advantage of the kindness of his
reception of me became quite unbearable. I felt a
passionate longing to see him again, to ask his pardon
for my deception. I wished to tell him who I was,

with what purpose I had gone to him and that I regretted it. But there was no need of a confession.
It would be enough to destroy the pages I had written
the night before. With this idea I arose. Before
tearing them up, I reread them. And then—any
writer will understand me—and then they seemed to
me so brilliant that I did not tear them up. Fauchery
is so intelligent, so generous, was the thought that
crossed my mind. What is there in this interview,
after all, to offend him? Nothing, absolutely nothing.
Even if I should go to him again this very morning,
tell him my story and that upon the success of my
little inquiry my whole future as a journalist might
depend? When he found that I had had five years of
poverty and hard work without accomplishing anything, and that I had had to go onto a paper in order
to earn the very bread I ate, he would pardon me,
he would pity me and he would say, "Publish your
interview." Yes, but what if he should forbid my
publishing it? But no, he would not do that.

I passed the morning in considering my latest plan.
A certain shyness made it very painful to me. But
it might at the same time conciliate my delicate
scruples, my "amour-propre" as an ambitious chron-
icler, and the interests of my pocket-book. I knew
that Pascal had the name of being very generous with
an interview article if it pleased him. And besides,
had he not promised me a reward if I succeeded with
Fauchery? In short, I had decided to try my experiment, when, after a hasty breakfast, I saw, on stepping
into the carriage I had had the night before, a victoria
with coat-of-arms drive rapidly past and was stunned
at recognizing Fauchery himself, apparently lost in a
gloomy revery that was in singular contrast to his

high spirits of the night before. A small trunk on the coachman's seat was a sufficient indication that he was going to the station. The train for Paris left in twelve minutes, time enough for me to pack my things pell-mell into my valise and hurriedly to pay my bill. The same carriage which was to have taken me to the Château de Proby carried me to the station at full speed, and when the train left I was seated in an empty compartment opposite the famous writer, who was saying to me, "You, too, deserting Nemours? Like me, you work best in Paris."

The conversation begun in this way, might easily have led to the confession I had resolved to make. But in the presence of my unexpected companion I was seized with an unconquerable shyness, moreover he inspired me with a curiosity which was quite equal to my shyness. Any number of circumstances, from a telegram from a sick relative to the most common-place matter of business, might have explained his sudden departure from the château where I had left him so comfortably installed the night before. But that the expression of his face should have changed as it had, that in eighteen hours he should have become the careworn, discouraged being he now seemed, when I had left him so pleased with life, so happy, so assiduous in his attentions to that pretty girl, Mademoiselle de Russaie, who loved him and whom he seemed to love, was a mystery which took complete possession of me, this time without any underlying professional motive. He was to give me the key before we reached Paris. At any rate I shall always believe that part of his conversation was in an indirect way a confidence. He was still unstrung by the unexpected incident which had caused both his hasty departure and the sudden metamorphosis in what he himself, if he had been writing, would have called his "intimate heaven." The story he told me was "per sfogarsi," as Bayle loved to say; his idea was that I would not discover the real hero. I shall always believe that it was his own story under another name, and I love to believe it because it was so exactly his way of looking at things. It was apropos of the supposed subject of my novel—oh, irony!—apropos of the real subject of my interview that he began.

"I have been thinking about our conversation and about your book, and I am afraid that I expressed myself badly yesterday. When I said that one may love and be loved at any age I ought to have added that sometimes this love comes too late. It comes when one no longer has the right to prove to the loved one how much she is loved, except by love's sacrifice. I should like to share with you a human document, as they say to-day, which is in itself a drama with a dénouement. But I must ask you not to use it, for the secret is not my own." With the assurance of my discretion he went on: "I had a friend, a companion of my own age, who, when he was twenty, had loved a young girl. He was poor, she was rich. Her family separated them. The girl married some one else and almost immediately afterward she died. My friend lived. Some day you will know for yourself that it is almost as true to say that one recovers from all things as that there is nothing which does not leave its scar. I had been the confidant of his serious passion, and I became the confidant of the various affairs that followed that first ineffaceable disappointment. He felt, he inspired, other loves. He tasted other joys. He endured other sorrows, and yet when we were alone and when we touched upon those confidences that come from the heart's depths, the girl who was the ideal of his twentieth year reappeared in his words. How many times he has said to me, 'In others I have always looked for her and as I have never found her, I have never truly loved any one but her.' "

"And had she loved him?" I interrupted.

"He did not think so," replied Fauchery. "At least she had never told him so. Well, you must now imagine my friend at my age or almost there. You must picture him growing gray, tired of life and convinced that he had at last discovered the secret of peace. At this time he met, while visiting some relatives in a country house, a mere girl of twenty, who was the image, the haunting image of her whom he had hoped to marry thirty years before. It was one of those strange resemblances which extend from the color of the eyes to the 'timber' of the voice, from the smile to the thought, from the gestures to the finest feelings of the heart. I could not, in a few disjointed phrases describe to you the strange emotions of my friend. It would take pages and pages to make you understand the tenderness, both present and at the same time retrospective, for the dead through the living; the hypnotic condition of the soul which does not know where dreams and memories end and present feeling begins; the daily commingling of the most unreal thing in the world the fantom of a lost love, with the freshest, the most actual, the most irresistibly naïve and spontaneous thing in it, a young girl. She comes, she goes, she laughs, she sings, you go about with her in the intimacy of country life, and at her side walks one long dead. After two weeks of almost

careless abandon to the dangerous delights of this
inward agitation imagine my friend entering by chance
one morning one of the less frequented rooms of the
house, a gallery, where, among other pictures, hung
a portrait of himself, painted when he was twenty-five.
He approaches the portrait abstractedly. There had
been a fire in the room, so that a slight moisture
dimmed the glass which protected the pastel, and on
this glass, because of this moisture, he sees distinctly
the trace of two lips which had been placed upon the
eyes of the portrait, two small delicate lips, the
sight of which makes his heart beat. He leaves
the gallery, questions a servant, who tells him that
no one but the young woman he has in mind has been
in the room that morning."

"What then?" I asked, as he paused.

"My friend returned to the gallery, looked once
more at the adorable imprint of the most innocent,
the most passionate of caresses. A mirror hung near
by, where he could compare his present with his former
face, the man he was with the man he had been. He
never told me and I never asked what his feelings
were at that moment. Did he feel that he was too
culpable to have inspired a passion in a young girl
whom he would have been a fool, almost a criminal,
to marry? Did he comprehend that through his age
which was so apparent, it was his youth which this
child loved? Did he remember, with a keenness that
was all too sad, that other, who had never given him
a kiss like that at a time when he might have returned
it? I only know that he left the same day, determined
never again to see one whom he could no longer
love as he had loved the other, with the hope, the
purity, the soul of a man of twenty."

A few hours after this conversation, I found myself once more in the office of the Boulevard, seated in Pascal's den, and he was saying, "Already? Have you accomplished your interview with Pierre Fauchery?"

"He would not even receive me," I replied, boldly.

"What did I tell you?" he sneered, shrugging his big shoulders. "We'll get even with him on his next volume. But you know, Labarthe, as long as you continue to have that innocent look about you, you can't expect to succeed in newspaper work."

I bore with the ill-humor of my chief. What would he have said if he had known that I had in my pocket an interview and in my head an anecdote which were material for a most successful story? And he has never had either the interview or the story. Since then I have made my way in the line where he said I should fail. I have lost my innocent look and I earn my thirty thousand francs a year, and more. I have never had the same pleasure in the printing of the most profitable, the most brilliant article that I had in consigning to oblivion the sheets relating my visit to Nemours. I often think that I have not served the cause of letters as I wanted to, since, with all my laborious work I have never written a book. And yet when I recall the irresistible impulse of respect which prevented me from committing toward a dearly loved master a most profitable but infamous indiscretion, I say to myself, "If you have not served the cause of letters, you have not betrayed it." And this is the reason, now that Fauchery is no longer of this world, that it seems to me that the time has come for me to relate my first interview. There is none of which I am more proud.

OUR LADY'S JUGGLER

By ANATOLE FRANCE

In the days of King Louis there lived a poor juggler by the name of Barnabas, a native of Compiègne, who wandered from city to city performing tricks of skill and prowess.

On fair days he would lay down in the public square a worn and aged carpet, and after having attracted a group of children and idlers by certain amusing remarks which he had learned from an old juggler, and which he invariably repeated in the same fashion without altering a word, he would assume the strangest postures, and balance a pewter plate on the tip of his nose. At first the crowd regarded him with indifference, but when, with his hands and head on the ground he threw into the air and caught with his feet six copper balls that glittered in the sunlight, or when, throwing himself back until his neck touched his heels, he assumed the form of a perfect wheel and in that position juggled with twelve knives, he elicited a murmur of admiration from his audience, and small coins rained on his carpet.

Still, Barnabas of Compiègne, like most of those who exist by their accomplishments, had a hard time making a living. Earning his bread by the sweat of his brow, he bore rather more than his share of those miseries we are all heir to through the fault of our Father Adam.

Besides, he was unable to work as much as he would have liked, for in order to exhibit his wonderful talents, he required—like the trees—the warmth of the sun and the heat of the day. In winter time he was no more than a tree stripped of its leaves, in fact, half-dead. The frozen earth was too hard for the juggler. Like the cicada mentioned by Marie de France, he suffered during the bad season from hunger and cold. But, since he had a simple heart, he suffered in silence.

He had never thought much about the origin of wealth nor about the inequality of human conditions. He firmly believed that if this world was evil the next could not but be good, and this faith upheld him. He was not like the clever fellows who sell their souls to the devil; he never took the name of God in vain; he lived the life of an honest man, and tho he had no wife of his own, he did not covet his neighbor's, for woman is the enemy of strong men, as we learn by the story of Samson which is written in the Scriptures.

Verily, his mind was not turned in the direction of ~~nal~~ desire, and it caused him far greater pain to ~~ce~~ drinking than to forego the pleasure of ~~For, tho he was not a drunkard, he enjoyed~~ ~~hen~~ the weather was warm. He was a good ~~God~~, and devout in his adoration of ~~When~~ he went into a church he never ~~the~~ image of the Mother of God ~~th~~ this prayer:

~~ver~~ my life until it shall please ~~en~~ I am dead, see that I have

~~day~~ of rain, as he walked sad ~~g~~ balls under his arm and his knives wrapped up in his old carpet seeking some barn where he might go supperless to bed, he saw a monk going in his direction, and respectfully saluted him. As they were both walking at the same pace, they fell into conversation.

"Friend," said the monk, "how does it happen that you are dressed all in green? Are you perchance going to play the part of the fool in some mystery?"

"No, indeed, father," said Barnabas. "My name is Barnabas, and my business is that of juggler. It would be the finest calling in the world if I could eat every day."

"Friend Barnabas," answered the monk, "be careful what you say. There is no finer calling than the monastic. The priest celebrates the praise of God, the Virgin, and the saints; the life of a monk is a perpetual hymn to the Lord."

And Barnabas replied: "Father, I confess I spoke like an ignorant man. My estate cannot be compared to yours, and tho there may be some merit in dancing and balancing a stick with a denier on top of it on the end of your nose, it is in no wise compara[ble] to your merit. Father, I wish I might, like yo[u] the Office every day, especially the Office of t[he] Holy Virgin, to whom I am specially a[ttached and] devoted. I would willingly give up the [art by which] I am known from Soissons to Beauva[is, in more than] six hundred cities and villages, i[n order to lead the] monastic life."

The monk was touched by [the sincerity of the] juggler, and as he was not lac[king in discernment, he] recognized in Barnabas one of [those men of good-will] of whom Our Lord has said, "[Peace be with them] on earth." And he made ans[wer]

"Friend Barnabas, come with me and I will see that you enter the monastery of which I am the Prior. He who led Mary the Egyptian through the desert put me across your path in order that I might lead you to salvation."

Thus did Barnabas become a monk. In the monastery which he entered, the monks celebrated most magnificently the cult of the Holy Virgin, each of them bringing to her service all the knowledge and skill which God had given him.

The Prior, for his part, wrote books, setting forth, according to the rules of scholasticism, all the virtues of the Mother of God. Brother Maurice copied these treatises with a cunning hand on pages of parchment, while Brother Aléxandre decorated them with delicate miniatures representing the Queen of Heaven seated on the throne of Solomon, with four lions on guard at the foot of it. Around her head, which was encircled by a halo, flew seven doves, the seven gifts of the Holy Spirit: fear, piety, knowledge, power, judgment, intelligence, and wisdom. With her were six golden-haired virgins: Humility, Prudence, Retirement, Respect, Virginity, and Obedience. At her feet two little figures, shining white and quite naked, stood in suppliant attitudes. They were souls imploring, not in vain, Her all-powerful intercession for their salvation. On another page Brother Aléxandre depicted Eve in the presence of Mary, that one might see at the same time sin and its redemption, woman humiliated, and the Virgin exalted. Among the other much-prized pictures in his book were the Well of Living Waters, the Fountain, the Lily, the Moon, the Sun, and the Closed Garden, of which much is said

in the Canticle; the Gate of Heaven and the City of
God. These were all images of the Virgin.

Brother Marbode, too, was one of the cherished
children of Mary. He was ever busy cutting images
of stone, so that his beard, his eyebrows and his hair
were white with the dust, and his eyes perpetually
swollen and full of tears. But he was a hardy and
a happy man in his old age, and there was no doubt
that the Queen of Paradise watched over the declining
days of Her child. Marbode represented Her seated
in a pulpit, Her forehead encircled by a halo, with
an orb of pearls. He was at great pains to make the
folds of Her robe cover the feet of Her of whom the
prophet has said, "My beloved is like a closed garden."

At times he represented Her as a graceful child, and
Her image seemed to say, "Lord, Thou art My Lord!"

There were also in the Monastery poets who composed prose writings in Latin and hymns in honor of
the Most Gracious Virgin Mary; there was, indeed,
one among them—a Picard—who translated the Miracles of Our Lady into rimed verses in the vulgar
tongue.

Perceiving so great a competition in praise and so
fine a harvest of good works, Barnabas fell to lament-
ing his ignorance and simplicity.

"Alas!" he sighed as he walked by himself one
day in the little garden shaded by the Monastery
wall, "I am so unhappy because I cannot, like my
brothers, give worthy praise to the Holy Mother of
God to whom I have consecrated all the love in my
heart. Alas, I am a stupid fellow, without art, and
for your service, Madame, I have no edifying ser-
mons, no fine treatises nicely prepared according to
the rules, no beautiful paintings, no cunningly carved

statues, and no verses counted off by feet and march-
ing in measure! Alas, I have nothing!"

Thus did he lament and abandon himself to his
misery.

One evening when the monks were talking together
by way of diversion he heard one of them tell of
a monk who could not recite anything but the *Ave
Maria*. He was scorned for his ignorance, but after
he died there sprang from his mouth five roses, in
honor of the five letters in the name Maria. Thus
was his holiness made manifest.

In listening to this story, Barnabas was conscious
once more of the Virgin's beneficence, but he was
not consoled by the example of the happy miracle,
for his heart was full of zeal and he wanted to celebrate the glory of His Lady in Heaven.

He sought for a way in which to do this, but in
vain, and each day brought him greater sorrow, until
one morning he sprang joyously from his cot and ran
to the chapel, where he remained alone for more than
an hour. He returned thither again after dinner, and
from that day onward he would go into the chapel
every day the moment it was deserted, passing the
greater part of the time which the other monks dedi-
cated to the pursuit of the liberal arts and the sci-
ences. He was no longer sad and he sighed no more.
But such singular conduct aroused the curiosity of
the other monks, and they asked themselves why
Brother Barnabas retired alone so often, and the
Prior, whose business it was to know everything that
the monks were doing, determined to observe Barnabas. One day, therefore, when Barnabas was alone
in the chapel, the Prior entered in company with

two of the oldest brothers, in order to watch, through the bars of the door, what was going on within.

They saw Barnabas before the image of the Holy Virgin, his head on the floor and his feet in the air, juggling with six copper balls and twelve knives. In honor of the Holy Virgin he was performing the tricks which had in former days brought him the greatest fame. Not understanding that he was thus putting his best talents at the service of the Holy Virgin, the aged brothers cried out against such sacrilege. The Prior knew that Barnabas had a simple soul, but he believed that the man had lost his wits. All three set about to remove Barnabas from the chapel, when they saw the Virgin slowly descend from the altar and, with a fold of her blue mantle, wipe the sweat that streamed over the juggler's forehead.

Then the Prior, bowing his head down to the marble floor, repeated these words:

"Blessed are the pure in heart, for they shall see God."

"Amen," echoed the brothers, bowing down to the floor.

E
P
his
nab
in